E&E

ELIOT & ELVIS

2 PLAYS

M.C. GARDNER

THE MAN FROM LLOYDS

&

A PRESLEY PASSION

ELIOT & ELVIS is printed in collaboration
with Another America.net

Printed in USA
ISBN-13: 978-0692470251

THE MAN FROM LLOYDS

ENACTMENT

THE MAN FROM LLOYDS:
1ST PERFORMANCE, VALDELAVILLA, SPAIN
OCTOBER 25, 2003
DIRECTOR: GREG STANFORD

DRAMATIS PERSONAE*

ACTOR A - T. S. ELIOT; WILD CAT COLOMBO; VOICE OF M. F. LLOYDS
ACTOR B - VIVIENNE ELIOT; VALERIE ELIOT; MADAME SOSOSTRIS
ACTOR C - MAURICE HAIGH-WOOD; ARCHDUKE FRANCIS; JFK
ACTOR D - BERTRAND RUSSELL; GAVRILO PRINCIP; L.H. OSWALD

* Each of the four cast members is called upon to play three roles. However, the various doppelgangers may be split into a baker's dozen of separate actors with little violence to the text. As in a dream of the. poet's poem—all the lines are those of the dreamer.

GLOSS

Thomas Stearns Eliot published *The Waste Land* in 1922. In it, Eliot explores the disillusion of the generation that survived the Great War and initiated the Jazz Age. *The Man from Lloyds* uses the poem to dramatize Eliot's relationship with his first wife, Vivienne Haigh-Wood and the memory of an impassioned friendship with Jean Verdenal, a French soldier killed in 1915. Also explored are the ramifications consequent to a "ménage"* involving Eliot, Vivienne and Bertrand Russell, during the war and Vivienne's subsequent committal to Northumberland Asylum in July of 1938.

Eliot's poem is divided into five parts: *The Burial of the Dead; The Game of Chess, The Fire Sermon; Death by Water;* and *What The Thunder Said.* The play follows this plan and disperses these five sections over two acts. **

After a brief prologue the play opens in Eliot's office at the London publishing house of Faber and Faber. This is depicted as an arch and cathedral window fronting the Proscenium Scrim. It is January 4, 1965 - the last day of Eliot's life. Eliot is told that "the *Man from Lloyds "* has arrived for the "deposition." The official from Lloyds Bank enters as a looming projected shadow on the Proscenium Scrim. Eliot invites him to sit and thereafter addresses the audience as if it was the *Man from Lloyds.* The Shadow will be seen again as the "electro-therapist," of Act 1; and as the "whip-master," of Act 2. The *Man from Lloyds* is investigating a claim of conscience. He is a projection from Eliot's psyche - he is Death. The play is framed by a pair of assassinations (Archduke Francis and his wife in Act 1 and JFK in Act 2). In Act 1, Eliot imagines Bertrand Russell as the Serbian Assassin, Gavrilo Princip; and the murdered Countess as his own wife, Vivienne. The Russell/Princip assassination is stylized with lighting, the freeze frame of stylized mimes, and a plain bench as the royal limousine. In the first act Eliot's voice is highly Anglicized - it is a voice of subterfuge and denial.

In Act 2 his voice is more confessional though remaining auricular. He imagines taking the sins of the world upon himself. Near the Act's end, the poet accepts a single-bolt *Mannlicher Carcano* from Russell/Oswald on the sixth floor of the Texas School Book Depository. The Act II assassination replicates the lighting of the assassination in Act 1. The plain bench is now the executive limousine of November 22, 1963. Eliot's shots correspond with the freeze frame of stylized mimes of the carnage on the stage. The final shot freezes and fades into history and darkness.

During his final "confession" his accent will return to the more natural patois of his Midwestern origins. Eliot's "mask," in Act 1, is the polished exterior he presented to the world. In Act 2 he applies makeup to a private, more interior face - the face of his doppelganger, Captain Colombo - the face of his Death Mask.***

NOTE ON THE MASKS:

Masks facilitate the multiple identities of the 4 cast members. Eliot may wear a black mask (Jolson) or smear an ash into a black cross on his forehead (Lent) for his rendition of "My Mammy." Russell wears a wolf-mask, wolf-tail and wolf claws during *Quarter to Nine/You Made Me Love You.* Each of the masks will be cut out around the mouth and chin to allow full vocal resonance. The only "realistic" masks are those of JFK, Marilyn Monroe, & Archduke Francis Ferdinand. The principals each don white masks to contrast with their funeral black suits for the finale of Act II.

NOTE ON THE HATS:

Headgear further differentiates the characters. Eliot and the *Man from Lloyds* wear identical Bowler Hats. Eliot's doppelganger, "Wild Cat" Colombo wears an oversize Stetson. Bertrand Russell favors a Top Hat. Maurice Haigh-Wood always has his Petty Officer's Hat near hand or head.

NOTE ON GUN SHOTS:

Four distinct concussions are employed. The gunshot connected with the death of Jean Verdenal echoes in the distance as if remembered in a dream. The gunshots that fell the Archduke and his wife issue from a silencer, the impacts are low decibel, sickening thuds. The "rat-ta-tat" of a machine gun (Hermes Pan homage) issues from the poet's cane during *Quarter to Nine/You Made Me Love You.* The three shots that close Act 1 and that repeat at the Kennedy Assassination, near the end of Act 2, are of increasingly louder volume until the final shot of each is a deafening concussion.

NOTE ON THE MUSIC:

Eliot was a contemporary of Al Jolson. The Jolson *Song Book* provides a lyrical accompaniment to the action of the play. The music of the Cantor's son is utilized in half of the play's fourteen scenes. The play opens with a recording of Jolson's *April Showers.* Eliot courts Vivienne with *I'm Sitting on Top of The World.* He later remembers his mother with a hybrid rendition of Berlin's *My Mammy.* He contemplates the perfidy of his wife with his former mentor, Bertrand Russell in *About a Quarter to Nine/You Made Me Love You.* A *cover* of *Swing Low, Sweet Chariot* companions JFK's coffin in Act II. A recording may substitute for the marching band described in the Finale. *Toot, Toot, Tootsie Goodbye* concludes the play. In *The Waste Land,* Eliot quotes from two of Wagner's operas: "The Sailor's Lament," from Act I *Tristan und Isolde* and "The Rhinemaidens Chorus," from Act III of *Gotterdammerung.* These will be operatically vocalized from recordings. Jean Verdenal was a fan of both these operas. Eliot dedicates "Prufrock And Other Observations" to his doomed friend: "For Jean Verdenal 1889-1915 mort aux Dardanelles." The Rhinemaidens of Wagner's *Ring Cycle* emerge as the mermaids of Eliot's *Prufrock.*

NOTE ON THE MARIES, MARYS & MARINAS.

Eliot's pet name of Marie/Mary for Vivienne is a play on Mary Magdalene of the Gospels and a conceit of the play. ****

*The "ménage" has been appraised differently by a variety of biographers of those in question. The reader is referred to Carole Seymour-Jones' *Painted Shadow* and to Russell's "fictional" confession in *Satan In the Suburbs*, for the terrain surveyed in the play.

** Lines from *The Waste Land* are numbered and italicized in the text of the play. Lines from other poems and plays are initialed, italicized and keyed to a note in the Appendix.

***In an early draft of the play I conjectured an Eliot doppelganger named Texas Bill. Texas Bill was as far from the buttoned-down persona of Eliot's public face as I could imagine. Rather than tweeds, cane and bowler, Texas Bill wore wear jeans, badge and Stetson. As the play neared completion *Painted Shadow* was published. In Carole Seymour-Jones' biography of Eliot's wife, Vivienne, she relates that Eliot did indeed have a doppelganger that the poet himself named and related to the pirate, Captain Colombo, of some youthful obscene poetry. Thereafter, Texas Bill was christened: Wild Cat Colombo of the Texas Rangers.

In 2005 the University of Texas published *Splendor in the Short Grass: The Grover Lewis Reader*. In it, Lewis remembers an evening out with fellow writer Larry McMurtry: "One night in a sports arena at SMU we witnessed the poet T. S. Eliot, visiting from England, just before his death, being solemnly invested as an honorary deputy sheriff of Dallas County, complete with badge and ten-gallon Stetson." Φ

****Any reader of the poet's collected works will note the number of Marys, Maries and Marinas found within its pages. I was struck that Oswald's wife was named Marina. I was astounded to discover that Officer Tippits' widow was named Marie.

Φ Lewis also related the irony of seeing T. S. Eliot in a venue that had featured Elvis Presley a night or two before.

ELIOT

THE MAN FROM LLOYDS
M.C. GARDNER

DONALD FREED
"il miglior fabbro"

PRE-PROLOGUE SCRIPT:

In the near intervening year between the Dallas death of JFK
and his own death of January 4, 1965,
T.S. Eliot became an honorary deputy sheriff of Dallas County, Texas
& was solemnly awarded an officer's badge and a ten-gallon Stetson
in a stadium presentation at Southern Methodist University.

PROLOGUE

SPOT on a MAN DOWN STAGE, next to a streetlamp, in front of the Proscenium Scrim. He is dressed in a three-piece suit and bowler hat. He is poised holding an umbrella with its point planted firmly on the ground.

<u>MUSIC CUE</u>: A scratchy "78" creaks out an old recording of Al Jolson's *April Showers*.

"Life is not a highway strewn with flowers,
Still it holds a goodly share of bliss,
When the sun gives way to April showers,
Here's the point you should never miss."

The man begins a simple lilting dance ...

"Though April showers may come your way,
They bring the flowers that bloom in May.
So if it's raining, have no regrets,
Because it isn't raining rain, you know,
(It's raining violets,)"

The wind of an approaching storm rises behind the Jolson recording.

"And where you see clouds upon the hills,
You soon will see crowds of daffodils,
So keep on looking for a blue bird,
And list'ning for his song,
Whenever April showers come along ..."

The song and the man fade into DARKNESS

The wind continues to rise.

It culminates in a wolf-cry and a peal of thunder.

SPOT on the same **MAN** *sans* hat, umbrella, and streetlamp. He is on bent knees with outstretched hands. His manner suggests prayer, crucifixion, and the showmanship of Al Jolson:

MAN:
Holy Father, I am not worthy of thy servants, nor their ministrations. *All my life they have been coming, these feet*[MC] even now making their way along the avenue. I know that death is a patient assignation – he may sabotage the heart, delay a doctor's aide or whistle down the wind of a Presidential Motorcade. Holy Mother, I am a miscreant flush full of sin and evil warrant. I await the disposition of thy Son, Christ Jesus.

    (MAN stands, defiantly.)

MAN (CONT'D):
He and he alone will judge me. No one else.
None other!

    (Surprised at the force of his demand, he concludes, humbly - dropping to his knee.)

MAN (CONCLUDING):
Even unto these, the waning hours of my life...

    MUSIC CUE: The recorded song returns:

    "So keep on looking for that bluebird
    and listening for its song,
    Whenever April Showers come along..."

He genuflects and bows his head.

The song fades.

Dim spot.

DARKNESS.

ACT I

SCENE 1: THE DEPOSITION

Lights up in office. The office is depicted as a simple Gothic arch that is lowered with and in front of the Proscenium Scrim.

A date is projected within the arch on the scrim.

DATE STAMP:
JANUARY 4, 1965 - LONDON, ENGLAND

The last day of T. S. ELIOT'S life.
The date Fades.
It is replaced with the inscription:

FABER & FABER, LTD.
T. STEARNS ELIOT, DIR. LONDON

The inscription fades. Enter ACTOR A, the *MAN* earlier seen in prayer. He is T. S. ELIOT. He stands in front of the left side of the arch. Enter Actor B. She is Eliot's 2nd wife, VALERIE FLETCHER ELIOT. She wears glasses and her hair, up. She stands in front of the right side of the arch.

They face forward and address each other as if from different rooms. ELIOT is lost in thought.

VALERIE FLETCHER ELIOT:
Someone to see you Tom...

T.S. ELIOT (TO HIMESELF)
So many waiting, how many waiting... (24)

VALERIE FLETCHER ELIOT:
The Man from Lloyds is here for the deposition ...

T. S. ELIOT (TO HIMSELF):
Between the conception and the creation. (HM)

VALERIE FLETCHER ELIOT:
Tom, shall I send him in?

T. S. ELIOT (TO HIMSELF):
between the emotion and the response...(HM)

VALERIE FLETCHER ELIOT:
Tom?

T. S. ELIOT (TO HIMSELF):
falls the shadow (HM)

> (A shadow is projected upon the Proscenium
> Scrim. It is dressed exactly as the poet, [ref.
> appendix] In addition to the three-piece suit and
> bowler hat, the shadow holds an umbrella and a
> brief case. It enlarges as it approaches. ELIOT
> checks his pocket watch.

T. S. ELIOT:
Fourth of January. Yes, Val - he's on the minute.

> VALERIE EXITS.
>
> FADE SHADOW.
>
> ELIOT WALKS FORWARD.
>
> HE ADDRESSES THE AUDIENCE
>
> > (AS IF THE AUDIENCE
> > WAS THE ARRIVING SHADOW,
> > THE MAN FROM LLOYDS).

T. S. ELIOT (TO MAN FROM LLOYDS):
Please, sit down. Would you care for a Gauloises? No? Perhaps tea? No, again? You are a proper puritan, properly pure, no doubt. This century would smash without its stimulations.

(**A CLOCK CHIMES**. ELIOT lifts a pill-cup.)

T. S. ELIOT (CONT'D TO MAN FROM LLOYDS):
I would, as well, but my heart's assured its rhythm if I'm mindful of that chime. I once worked for your firm. (PAUSE) That won't save me?

> (ELIOT takes a drag on his cigarette.
> He begins to violently cough and gag.
> He steadies himself, catching his breath.)

T. S. ELIOT(CONT'D):
No, (PAUSE) I didn't imagine it would. (PAUSE) *Morals & Ethics Division?* — you've requested documents four decades in the distance, yet, the detritus of memory remains reasonably intact. Ah, you have a form, how helpful. Birth date? September 26, 1888. Matriculation? Harvard, 1906. Dissertation? Yes, on F. H. Bradley's *Appearance and Reality.* Doctorate? No, the war intervened. My wife, Valerie? No, of course, you mean the first Mrs. Eliot - Vivienne *Marie* Haigh-Wood. Marie was a pet name known only to myself and a select coterie of others. We were married June 26, 1915 — it was the occasion of my subsequent placement with Lloyds. Vivienne Marie, my lovely Magdalene. She of the fens, the downs and the sea-swept towns of my youth and youthful yearning. My first World War, my first World Wife—each a cataclysm of the first order. I'm sorry, the Bank has compiled an extensive query in which levity is ill-suited. Please forgive an old grammarian his rhetorical flair. Employment during the war? As I said, Lloyds Bank - 1917. Yes, Bowler hat and all. It was the occasion of some mirth by Huxley down in Bloomsbury.

> (ELIOT picks up a Saturday Evening Post.
> Norman Rockwell's Memorial Portrait of JFK
> appears on the cover [ref. appendix]. The portrait
> is projected on the Rear Screen.)

T. S. ELIOT (CONT'D TO MAN FROM LLOYDS):
Did you know that Huxley expired the same day as Kennedy?
John Fitzgerald *Fisher King*...

> (A loud echoing clang is heard.
> ELIOT glances at the walls,
> suspiciously, and then continues.)

T. S. ELIOT (CONT'D):
and the last of the *Bloomsberries* blasted to atoms and tossed to the pit. Now, as to the episode of which you inquire, my wife - that is Valerie and I, were in New York toward the end of '63. We arranged to visit my childhood home - My*cenae on the Missouri,* just outside St. Louis. Val returned to London, shortly after the Assassination. Myself? I'd planned to stay through the 3rd week of December. On the 16th I attended an early morning Mass. Something in the wafer or something in the wine lingered on through Sunday as if a dreadful harlequin or mime. I was afflicted by voices - familiar, yet strange. A malady I'd not encountered since my "treatments" in Lausanne.

(LIGHTS DOWN on ELIOT}.

SCENE 2: THE SÉANCE

DATE STAMP:

DECEMBER 16, 1963
MYCENAE ON THE MISSOURI

Through the scrim we see the rising radiance of a crystal ball. It illuminates a portion of the primary stage set: a series of columns suggesting the ruin of a Doric Temple. VIVIENNE HAIGH-WOOD sits alone at a table with her hand extended to the left as if being held by someone unseen. ACTOR C, in military fatigues and officer's hat, pours himself a potent libation, then exits with the bottle. The woman is played by the same actor (ACTOR B) who played VALERIE in the earlier scene. She wears her hair down and doesn't wear glasses. A stuffed parrot, MR. APOLLINAX, sits on a perch, to the side.

VIVIENNE HAIGH-WOOD:
The chair she sat on like a burnished throne, glowed on the marble . . . [77, 78]

(SPOT ON ELIOT)

T. S. ELIOT (TO MAN FROM LLOYDS):
The same woman? I see you've read *The Waste Land's* "Notes" Ezra wagered five and twenty I'd not in my lifetime meet a handful who had. *"So all the women are the same woman ... and what Tiresias sees is the substance of the poem."* [N] The *Notes* by rote! You are a scary fellow. Yes, as you've surmised, she's the first Mrs. Eliot, Vivienne Haigh-Wood, dead now, near 18 years. A natural death? Why are you staring at me? Her death was more natural than her life. Lloyds handled the probate. If you doubt me you need only consult your records. The man who departed with my favorite *Single Malt*? That was Vivienne's baby brother, Maurice Haigh-Wood.

(MORE)

25

T.S. ELIOT (CONTD)
He prefers his *formula, undiluted* over ice. Yes, he's well along in his *cups* for this hour of the morning. The man on the left? I can't quite make him out. Is he wearing a Stetson? That would be Captain W.C. Colombo of the Austin Texas Rangers. Dreadful man, perfectly dreadful. The W.C.? A sobriquet for *Wild Cat* when he's on the peep and prowl. He's on extended leave from the constabulary but he supplements his income with popcorn sales and a partnership in a local cinema—*The Texas Theater,* in Dallas.

> (ELIOT begins his transition into his dark doppelganger, WILD CAT COLOMBO. Whereas it is Eliot's intention to be **saved** it is Wild Cat's intention to be **lost** in his desires wherever they might lead——devil be damned! Scrim up. He puts on an oversize Stetson. He joins MADAME SOSOSTRIS/VIVIENNE at the Séance table. She remains deep in a trace. ELIOT removes his glasses. The transformation is complete. He takes MADAME SOSOSRIS/VIVIENNE'S proffered hand. The séance continues.)

MADAME SOSOSTRIS/VIVIENNE:
-- the glass doubled the flames of seven branched candelabra reflecting the light upon the table.[82, 83]

APOLLINAX:
No, it didn't - squawwwwwwwk!

MADAME SOSOSTRIS/VIVIENNE:
Shush, Apollinax! The soon to die are little different than the newly dead - we are each the one and soon shall be the other.

> (We hear, again, the loud echoing clang. Each looks warily, about.)

MADAME SOSOSTRIS/VIVIENNE (CONT'D):
The fire within burns green and orange, framed by colored stones.[95]

(The crystal throws a **GREEN, ORANGE & RED** glow upon the ruins. We hear the howl of a wolf pack.)

WILD CAT/ELIOT:
Mommy walks her hellhounds searching for a bone.

APOLLINAX:
Full fathom five - We're all going to dieeeeeeeeeeee!

> (The hounds go silent. VIVIENNE begins to place her Tarot on the table.)

WILD CAT/ELIOT:
Madame Sosostris, I see you have a *wicked pack of cards.* (46)
I am -

MADAME SOSOSTRIS/VIVIENNE:
You are Captain Wild Cat Colombo with your *musical sounds and your Baskerville Hounds*(B) and your Lee Harvey Oswald pinched in your grand mezzanine.

> (The Texan Smiles. He picks up a card.)

WILD CAT/ELIOT:
The *Cardinal's Concubine.* You are no Madame, but the pagan playmate, she. You'd be as nasty a tart if you dressed for the part. I hope you'll soon play with me.

> (MADAME SOSOSTRIS/VIVIENNE rises to leave, but she is embraced by COLOMBO/ELIOT. She struggles in his grip and cries out:)

MADAME SOSOSTRIS/VIVIENNE:
Tom, help me!

27

WILD CAT/ELIOT:
My love you're a slut ...

> (He paws her breast and kisses her roughly on the
> neck. She pulls away, attempts to leave, but is
> blocked by him.)

WILD CAT/ELIOT (CONT'D):
Don't pretend you are not! *The slick Brazilian jaguar does not in its aboreal gloom distil so rank a feline smell as* Vivie *in her drawing room.*(W) Pity the waste of such a wanton. Your Tommy's as queer as a Bourbon Street leer. *The Jolly Tinker came across the sea with his four and twenty inches hanging to his knee.* (JT) You are a fading discard, Madame Vivienne Marie - the poet favors the boyish bosom of his new bride, Valerie. The bitch is now in heat - *his eight and forty inches drops nearly to his feet!*(JT)

APOLLINAX:
Ding, dong, doll—h*e's gone and fucked us all.* (JT) Squawwwk!

> (Lights down on all except COLOMBO. He
> hangs his Stetson on a nail. He puts his glasses on,
> returns to the persona of the poet, walks forward
> to the front of stage. Scrim down.)

T. S. ELIOT (TO MAN FROM LLOYDS):
I'm sorry. The "Jolly Tinker" poems were a product of my youth and not intended for public recital. As for the obscenity of the parrot - Vivie is responsible for the looseness of its language. Mr. Apollinax was named for Lord Bertrand Russell, the Nobel Laureate...

> (A photo of BERTRAND RUSSELL is projected
> on the Proscenium Scrim. He is dressed in elegant
> evening wear, top hat and tails.)

T. S. ELIOT (CONT'D):
he was less than lordly and rarely noble. In point of fact, he diminished my life!

28

VIVIENNE HAIGH-WOOOD (VO):
What shall I do now? What shall I do? What shall we ever do? (131,134)

T. S. ELIOT (CONT'D TO MAN FROM LLOYDS):
He abused my wife!

VIVIENNE HAIGH-WOOD (CONT'D VO):
I shall rush out as I am, and walk the street. With my hair down so! (132,133)

T. S. ELIOT (CONT'D)
Russell was awarded the Nobel Prize in 1950. I received mine in '48
by virtue of my verse...

> (Through the scrim a SPOT is directed on
> ACTOR D, BERTRAND RUSSELL. He is
> dressed [here and hereafter] as in the projected
> photo - in top hat and tails.)

BERTRAND RUSSELL:
The sword against my *lower leg was feeling bold & rooty.*
I *took* my *cock in both* my *hands and swore it was a beauty!* (CP)

> (Spot off RUSSELL and his photo.)

T. S. ELIOT (CONT'D TO MAN FROM LLOYDS):
I trust collegian ribaldries need not be entered into your report.
Their survival is a source of regrettable mischief. You're still taking
notes? Ah yes, strictly confidential. That is reassuring ... I
composed these, ah, "verses" shortly after my arrival at the
Sorbonne. I was twenty-two. Yes, it was about that time I met Jean,
Jean Verdenal.

> (The photograph of Jean Verdenal is
> projected on the Rear Screen.
>
> Theme, "Sailor's Lament"
> Wagner's *Tristan Und Isolde:)*

SAILOR (SINGING VO):
Frisch weht der Wind (31)
Der Heimat zu (32)

T. S. ELIOT:
We shared an innocence and an ardor that
only Paris could sustain ... I met Vivienne in March ... *April
is the cruelest month* ...(1)

(A shot is fired from afar.)

T. S. ELIOT (TO MAN FROM LLOYDS):
Jean was killed in May.

SAILOR (SINGING VO):
Mein Irisch Kind,(33)
Wo weilest du? (34)

A CLOCK CHIMES.

(The photo of Jean Verdenal, fades.
ELIOT discovers his pills are missing.)

T. S. ELIOT (CONT'D TO MAN FROM LLOYDS):
My pills? Mightn't I have a one? I see, only as needed.

(He drinks a glass of water. His hand shakes.
He has trouble resettling his glass.)

T. S. ELIOT (CONT'D TO MAN FROM LLOYDS):
Viv and I were married that June; a year, almost to the day of the
Archduke's Assassination. We courted at the Hammersnith *Palais de
Danse*. I was no *Astaire* but Vivie was all the rage. We called her the
"Hyacinth Girl," my lovelyy *Magdalene of the day*. Afterwards we'd
talk and walk along the quay...

(LIGHTS DOWN)

SCENE 3: GAVRILO PRINCIP

> **We see VIVIENNE through the mist of the scrim. Scrim up. ELIOT crosses the stage. He joins his first wife early in their courtship.**

VIVIENNE HAIGH-WOOD:
Tell me about America. Do the girls wear corn husks in their hair? Do they wash their face in buttermilk and drive cowboys to despair? Did they listen to their *teach*? Were they always in your reach? *Did* they *dare to eat* a *peach?* (LS)

T. S. ELIOT:
My little Mary, Mary, quite contrary ...

VIVIENNE HAIGH-WOOD:
"Mary had a little lamb whose fleece was white as snow." I'm not the Virgin Mother, Tom - which, of course, you know.

> ### MUSIC CUE:
> *I'm Sitting On Top Of The World*

T. S. ELIOT (SINGING):
Don't want any millions. I'm getting my share /
I've got only one suit that's all I can wear/
A bundle of money won't make you feel gay /
My sweet little honey is making me say...
We're sitting on top o~ the world /
Rolling along, just rolling along ...

> (The photo of BERTRAND RUSSELL is projected on the Rear Screen. ACTOR D, as RUSSELL / PRINCIP appears above and behind the duo. He is dressed in top hat and tails. He screws a silencer on a smallish handgun. As ELIOT imagines, his rival is about to murder the Archduke Francis Ferdinand and begin WWI.)

TOM AND VIV (SINGING):
Some people have diamonds and beautiful pearls /
While others have children with long hanging curls /
Keep all of your fortune, keep all of your fame /
We've got each other that's all we can claim."
Just like Humpty Dumpty waiting to fall /
We're sitting on top o~ the world /
Rolling along, just rolling along ...

(VIVIENNE and TOM "roll along" to an exit at STAGE
LEFT. DARKNESS Scrim down. Lights up under the arch
in front of Proscenium Scrim. ELIOT returns and continues
his discussion with THE MAN FROM LLOYDS:)

T. S. ELIOT (TO MAN FROM LLOYDS):
The man in the top hat is a scholar and student—an amalgam of
mentor and murder. In the tatter of my memory Russell's white
glove is also the "Black Hand" of, Gavrilo Princip. I'm told that,
although the "Great Man" was England's premier pacifist, he and
the assassin share a cheekbone and quite possibly a chin. The
Archduke was slain on a Sunday morning -- a *black mass* murder in a
motorcade - but it was not a requiem that was exclusively his own…

DATE STAMP:
JUNE 28, 1914--SARAJEVO, BOSNIA.

(Through shadows and Scrim, we see VIVIENNE as the
Countess, with a parasol & ACTOR C in a ROYAL MASK,
sitting on the last of three parallel benches—the back seat of a
"limousine", at STAGE RIGHT. The Countess whispers to the
Archduke. They both laugh.) Enter BERTRAND RUSSELL, in
top hat & tails—he wears a white glove on his left hand and a
black glove on his right. He holds a pistol in his right hand. He
walks up behind the ARCHDUKE & DUCHESS.
LIGHTING TURNS GREEN. RUSSELL fires a "muted"
shot to Archduke's back. The ARCHDUKE arches in shock
and then crumples off the bench to the floor. **LIGHTING
TURNS ORANGE.** He fires again. VIVIENNE leaves the
bench & tries to shield her "husband"—**FREEZE FRAME.)**

T. S. ELIOT:
It was reported that his wife, the Countess Chotek von Chotkova, was shot in the abdomen, while trying to shield her husband from the horror of the *Black Hand's* terrible slap.. The Archduke pleaded with his wife:

ARCHDUKE FRANCIS FERDINAND (ACTOR C):
"Sophie, dear! Sophie dear! - don't die, don't die for the sake of the children."

> (**LIGHTING TURNS RED**. RUSSELL fires two more "muted" shots to VIVIENNE'S abdomen & a kill-shot to the Archduke's chest. **FREEZE FRAME.** (The shots are low level impacts horribly imagined). **LIGHTS OFF** on Assassination.
>
> ELIOT feels a pointed jab to his heart. He staggers a step or two forward - he falls to his knees in pain, consequent to a heart attack.)

T. S. ELIOT:
Ahhhhhhh! My pills, God - my pills, goddamn you! Please, please...

> (ELIOT begs THE MAN FROM LLOYDS for his cardiac pills. He mimes receiving the desired pill and water as if a child at communion.)

T. S. ELIOT (HALTINGLY, TO MAN FROM LLOYDS):
Thank you, (PAUSE) their effectiveness is in direct proportion (PAUSE) to the perception (PAUSE) of their need. Bertrand Russell once suggested that happiness was only possible *before* the War. Yes, WWI, (PAUSE) the "GREAT WAR." Great and yet, (PAUSE) at times, it seems that only one man died ...

> (Sound of a distant gun shot.)

T. S. ELIOT (CONT'D):
whose name was Jean...

DARKNESS

FROM THE DARKNESS
A TITLE CARD EMERGES
ON THE PROSCENIUM SCRIM:

I
<u>THE BURIAL OF THE DEAD</u>

SCENE 4: THE URN

> The title card fades. Scrim and Lights up. The
> dawn is frozen in the East. The ruin of a
> European cityscape is projected on the Rear
> Screen. The temple is suffused with the red
> and shadowed lighting of a Wasteland. VIV
> and ELIOT stand in the center of temple.
> They face forward. They address each other as
> if from separate worlds.

VIVIENNE HAIGH-WOOD:
Excuse me. I hope somebody knows where I am because my
medicine is misbehaving.

T. S. ELIOT:
It's not your medication.

VIVIENNE HAIGH-WOOD:
Tom? You never came to (PAUSE)... to "Northumberland." How
is it I find you here? Where are we?

T. S. ELIOT:
This was once a garden, Viv - where paradise was lost.

VIVIENNE HAIGH-WOOD:
The trees are bare and the dead leaves stir across cracked
earth.

T. S. ELIOT:
Take care, Vivienne - *the leaves are full of children...*[BN]

CHORUS OF CHILDREN (VO):
Goosey, Goosey, gander whither shall I wander? Upstairs, downstairs, in the fields I saunter.

(Repeat and fade behind dialogue.)

VIVIENNE HAIGH-WOOD:
The children are hidden in the foliage. Each boy cloistered in a hedgerow— A mere abstraction of a lad.

(End nursery rhyme)

VIVIENNE HAIGH-WOOD (CONT'D):
I don't like your ancient garden, Tom. It makes me rather sad.

(VIVIENNE deposits her cigarette in a Grecian Urn.

The Urn is inscribed with a white rose.
It is projected on the Rear Screen.

The rose fades. She exits.

ELIOT walks a few steps closer to his audience.)

T. S. ELIOT (TO MAN FROM LLOYDS):
My own vices aside – sometimes smoking is more than nicotine yellowing lung and bone …

> **MUSIC CUE**:
> "Sailor's Lament" from
> Wagner's *Tristan Und Isolde* -

(More distantly afar...)

SAILOR (RECORDED VO):
Frisch weht der Wind [31] *Der Heimat Zu* [32]

T. S. ELIOT (CONT'D):
Sometimes two together is more than twice alone ...

VIVIENNE HAIGH-WOOD (VO):
My nerves are bad tonight. Stay with me. Speak to me ... Why do you never speak? Speak![111,112]

SAILOR (RECORDED VO):
Mein Irisch Kind [33] *Wo welest du?* [34]

> (ELIOT is frozen in place with his head cocked straining to hear the music through the recriminations.
>
> He picks up the Urn. He walks slowly, in a measured gait, to a pedestal at **STAGE LEFT**.
>
> He places the urn on the pedestal. He returns short of breath and slightly bent.
>
> After each return from his narrative he appears more decrepit. He places his hand over his heart checking its palpitations. He speaks haltingly.)

T. S. ELIOT (TO MAN FROM LLOYDS):
Why does *the day delay?* (PAUSE) *When will time fly away?* [FFE] Yes, there is a chill. (PAUSE) Valerie assembled the ensemble I'm in. *My morning coat and my collar mounting firmly to the chin,* (PAUSE) *my necktie rich and modest but asserted with a pin.* [LS]

> (He exits. Scrim down. DARKNESS. Through the Scrim: SPOT on the URN on pedestal, at STAGE LEFT. VIVIENNE enters. She approaches and picks up the URN.)
>
> The URN'S inscription is projected on the Scrim beneath a white rose:

VIVIENNE HAIGH-WOOD ELIOT

May 28, 1888 – November 22, 1947

(VIV drops the URN. SPOT on VIV at CENTER
STAGE. She crouches in terror. She slams her fist
against the floor,)

VIVIENNE HAIGH-WOOD:
No... Noooo... Dear God, Noooooooooo...

(**A RECORDED CHORUS** chants the word
"burning" - each repetition increasing in ferocity.)

CHORUS:
Burning! Burning! Burning, Burning! (308)

(The scrim writhes with the red glow of projected
fire. VIVIENNE mimes the torture of the flame.)

VIVIENNE HAIGH-WOOD:
Ahhhhhhhhhhhhhhhhhhhhhhhhhhhhhhhhhhhhhhhhhhhhh!

(She collapses. **DARKNESS.**
Lights slowly up, CENTER STAGE.
ELIOT cradles VIVIENNE at the foot of a
plain wooden cross. She is unconscious.
The pair is staged as a **"PIETA."**

T. S. ELIOT:
O lord thou pluckest me out (309)
O lord thou pluckest (310)

CHORUS (AS IF FROM AFAR):
b-u-r-n-i-n-g-g-g-g-g-g-g-g-g-g-g-g ... (311)

DARKNESS

(**ELIOT'S** voice breaks from the shadows...)

T. S. ELIOT (VO, IN A SOB):
I tried to save her. Save her from the Pythagorean paganism of that pious, megalomaniacal, Godless prig!

> (Lights up, STAGE LEFT. ELIOT is alone
> with the cross. Wearily, he removes his coat.
> He places it over an arm of the cross.)

T. S. ELIOT (CONT'D TO MAN FROM LLOYDS):
Her hysteria always followed the failure of her flesh. I borrowed and begged to pay for medication. But her ailment was beyond medicinal application ...

> (**A SCARLET ROBE AND MITER** is lowered
> from above. He lifts it and holds it to his cheek.)

T. S. ELIOT (CONT'D):
Only the tattered Robe of Christ Jesus could stave off the certainty of her damnation. Only the Imperial Red of his chosen emissaries could deliver her from a darkness...

> (Lights dim. SPOT illuminates BERTRAND RUSSELL
> in top hat, standing behind ELIOT and the cross -
> RUSSELL "lifts" the coat and exits to the wings.)

T. S. ELIOT (CONT'D):
growing in and with surety about her.

DARKNESS

SCENE 5: PEEPING TOMMY

The headline: "DULLES JOINS WARREN COMMISSION" is projected on the Rear Screen. Lights up, CENTER STAGE. ACTOR C, MAURICE HAIGH-WOOD (in military fatigues and officer's hat) and ACTOR D, BERTRAND RUSSELL (in top hat) enter as a *CHORUS* WITH NEWSPAPERS.

MAURICE HAIGH-WOOD:
The first thing to do is to form the committees...[C]

BERTRAND RUSSELL:
Two pounds a week with a bonus as pretty.[C]

MAURICE HAIGH-WOOD:
A commission has been appointed and bled...[C]

BERTRAND RUSSELL:
The patsy has been anointed though dead!

(They toss their respective papers in the trash and exit. ELIOT and VIVIENNE enter at STAGE RIGHT and LEFT. ELIOT wears **THE IMPERIAL RED AND MITER OF A CARDINAL** They each face forward. A coffin is illuminated between them).

T. S. ELIOT (TO MAN FROM LLOYDS):
The purported "sole" assassin never stood alone.

VIVIENNE HAIGH-WOOD (IN A COCKNEY ACCENT):
He do the Police in different voices... [WLE]

T. S. ELIOT:
The undetermined prints on Oswald's rifle are our own.

VIVIENNE HAIGH-WOOD:
Stay with me. Speak to me... [111, 112]

(ELIOT walks to the coffin.
He pulls a black glove over
his right hand.)

DATE STAMP:
JANUARY 22, 1947 –
NORTHUMBERLAND ASYLUM MORTUARY.

VIVIENNE HAIGH-WOOD:

Before the fires fed upon me, they put me in a box. *At my back, in a cold blast I heard the rattle of bones ...*

> (ELIOT takes hold of the raised
> lid of the coffin.)

VIVIENNE HAIGH-WOOD:

and chuckle spread from ear to ear as Tom... (185,186)

> (ELIOT violently closes the coffin!)

VIVIENNE HAIGH-WOOD (CONT'D):

latched the darkness down!

> (The loud metallic clang, heard earlier in his office
> and at the séance, reverberates on the sound system.)

VIVIENNE HAIGH-WOOD (CONT'D):

We had no children. Tom didn't fancy them - unless you count the danseurs of the Ballets Russes. It's alright, Tommy - you can only properly kill a girl once.

> (**DARKNESS**. Scrim down. Lights up on ELIOT
> under his office arch. **ELIOT IS STILL IN HIS**
> **CARDINAL ROBES.** He takes off the **MITER**.)

T. S. ELIOT (TO MAN FROM LLOYDS):

What she meant? Vivienne was cryptic to the point of being elliptic. Yes, we talked of having a family. She wanted her *first* to be a girl. She bought a bolt of pink gingham from Chelsea and begged my mother for an heirloom lace that was nonpareil. A game that went too far? At the time I didn't see the harm in naming children born only in her mind. I had my verse - she had poetry of her own. We finally settled on a name. Yes, Marina. How did you know? That's right, Marina after Shakespeare's *Pericles.* Quite the only thing of value in the play. *"What seas, what shores what grey rocks and what islands, what water lapping bow and scent of pine and the wood thrush singing through the fog. What images return.* **O my daughter . . .** *"* (M)

(ELIOT removes his glasses. He appears diminished by the memory. He brushes a tear from his eye.

A confessional screen is lowered from above. He puts the **MITER** back on his head. Enter VIVIENNE, on opposite side of screen. ELIOT is her **FATHER CONFESSOR.** They both sit.)

VIVIENNE HAIGH-WOOD:
Forgive me, Father. I am newlywed - but Tom and I sleep in different beds. He rarely comes to me. Marriage is not what I thought – not what I thought at all. I married Tom in summer - I betrayed him in the fall.

(ELIOT stands and begins nervously pacing back and forth like a trapped animal.)

VIVIENNE HAIGH-WOOD (CONT'D):
The blood upon the sheets suggested that I was touched by more than I should know ...

(VIVIENNE begins to titter, hysterically.)

VIVIENNE HAIGH-WOOD (CONT'D):
Bertie wasn't bothered by my menstrual flow.

T. S. ELIOT:
AHHHHHHHHHHHEEEEEEEEEEEEEEEEEEEEEEEEEEE EEEEEEEEEEEE!

(VIVIENNE is startled by the violence of the scream. She takes a step or two back. She puts her hand to her mouth in fear. ELIOT regains his composure. He returns to the demeanor of her CONFESSOR.)

T. S. ELIOT (TO VIVIENNE):
Child - Daughter, the "Marys" are sufficient to the day. Sin no more and go thy way ...

(VIVIENNE exits. Confessional Screen up.)

DATE STAMP:
NOVEMBER 22, 1921 - DR. ROGER VITTOZ, PSYCHOLOGIST

(LOUD CRACKLE OF ELECTRICITY.
VIVIENNE'S voice is heard on the sound system.)

VIVIENNE (VO):
It's time, Tom - that's a good lamb ...

(Lower a large facsimile of Francis Bacon's "SCREAMING POPE INNOCENT X". ELIOT sits in the same rigid pose as the Bacon portrait. Enter BERTRAND RUSSELL, [ACTOR D in top hat]. He straps ELIOT to the chair. ELIOT'S fingers dance nervously on the ends of the chair arms. The shadow of THE MAN FROM LLOYDS looms upon the scrim. He speaks with ELIOT'S voice.)

MAN FROM LLOYDS (ELIOT'S RECORDED VOICE):
Let's see. It says here that you wedded her in June and Russell bedded the remains. Is that accurate?

T. S. ELIOT:
I wooed her and won her and then the Devil came...

(On the Proscenium Scrim, THE MAN FROM LLOYDS pulls a switch. Lights dim. We hear the **LOUD CRACKLE OF ELECTRICITY.** ELIOT bolts upright in Vittoz's **"ELECTRIC CHAIR."**)

T. S. ELIOT:
OWWWWWWWWWWWWWWWWWWWWWWWWWWEEEEE
EEEEEE!

MAN FROM LLOYDS (SUPPRESSED AMUSEMENT):
Hmmm. It would appear that your betrothal and her betrayal -
why, they scarcely missed a beat...

T. S. ELIOT:
It was then that the voices rose and started to repeat.

> (THE MAN FROM LLOYDS turns up the voltage.
> Lights dim. The **ELECTRICAL CRACKLE** is louder.
>
> ELIOT strains against the teeth-shattering
> current.)

T. S. ELIOT:
OWWWWWWWWWWWWWWWWWWWWWWWWWWWWEE
EEEEEEEEEEEEEEEEEEEEEEEEEE!

MAN FROM LLOYDS (RECORDED VO):
Whispered they of good or whispered they of ill?

T. S. ELIOT:
The only word they whispered was to **KILL!** to **KILL!** to **KILL!**

> (On the Proscenium Scrim, THE MAN FROM
> LLOYDS administers a final blast of "therapy."
> The lights dim. ELIOT is, again, jolted upright in
> his chair as the..**ELECTRICITY ARCS**
> **ABOVE HIS HEAD. SMOKE AND SPARKS**
> **FLY OUT FROM THE BOTTOM OF THE**
> **CHAIR.**

T. S. ELIOT:
OWWWWWWWWWWWWWWWWWWWWWWWWWWEEEE
EEEEEEEEEEEEEEEEEEEEEEE!

(He grips the arms of the chair and strains upward mirroring the iconography of Frances Bacon's **"POPE INNOCENT X"** series. THE MAN FROM LLOYDS turns off the voltage. ELIOT slumps unconscious in his chair. **DARKNESS**.)

VIVIENNE (FROM THE DARKNESS):
All done, Tommy – you'll soon be right as rain...

(Lights up. RUSSELL unfastens the straps on the chair. He pinches ELIOT'S cheeks. He passes smelling salts under the poet's nose. ELIOT twitches and slowly revives. He stands and painfully removes the Cardinal robes and miter. He hands the costume to BERTRAND RUSSELL. RUSSELL exits. ELIOT walks forward to a glass of water. He drinks and seems to regain a measure of strength. He continues his deposition with THE MAN FROM LLOYDS)

T. S. ELIOT (VO TO MAN FROM LLOYDS):
The costume? Yes, *Murder In The Cathedral.* I didn't think Vivienne would mind. They both knew that I knew. They believed I was inclined.

(**A CLOCK CHIMES**. VIVIENNE enters. She holds a whip. With each crack of the whip, ELIOT becomes increasingly agitated.)

VIVIENNE HAIGH-WOOD:
So you've been peeping. (CRACK OF WHIP) Bloody peeping Tommy. I know something of death, Tom - courtesy of lessons learned in lockup. (CRACK OF WHIP) You fuck with death and it will damn well fuck with you. Now that I'm dead I must live with my sins - whatever depth or depravation. (CRACK OF WHIP) If it's any consolation, Bertie's *caresses were unreproved if undesired. His hands encountered no defense. His vanity required no response and made a welcome of indifference* - much like your own. [237, 236, 239, 240, 241, 242]

(VIVIENNE cracks the riding
stock. The sound of the whip
allows a little of the repressed
Texan to break through.
ELIOT slaps on his Stetson.
He thrusts his hips forward
miming a fevered rut.)

ELIOT/WILD CAT:

She *jack-knifed upward at the knees then straightened out from heel to hip pushing the framework of the bed and clawing at the pillow slip!* (SWE)

(ELIOT stops abruptly. He removes hat .He is
shamed. in the gaze of THE MAN FROM
LLOYDS. He continues, sickened at his display
and the memory of the "ménage.")

T. S. ELIOT

and I would sit at the foot of the stair and flog myself until I bled - there would not be a word to say. You would love me because I should have strangled you ... (SEBASTIAN)

VIVIENNE HAIGH-WOOD:

and I should love you the more because I mangled you. (SEBASTIAN)

T. S. ELIOT:

Vivienne, please!

(She sits. She lays out her Tarot.)

VIVIENNE HAIGH-WOOD:

Tom, Bertrand *carries something on his back which I was forbidden* to *see.*
(56, 53, 54)

(She turns over the last card and gasps.)

VIVIENNE HAIGH-WOOD (CONT'D):

Tommy, *he's the One-eyed merchant!* (52)

DARKNESS

SCENE 6: MAMMY

Lights Up Slowly. ELIOT is under the office arch with THE MAN FROM LLOYDS.

T. S. ELIOT (TO MAN FROM LLOYDS):
Russell sensed that Viv was bored - bed and board! The bastard knew exactly what he was about and then he went about it.

While I knelt before the altar to finish my report –
He diddled Vivi in the cloister purely for the sport!

> (Lights dim. In a distant echoing voice, THE MAN FROM LLOYDS speaks a liturgical line from the **LATIN GLORIA:** *Who Sits At The Right Hand Of The Father. Have Mercy On Us*)

MAN FROM LLOYDS (ELIOT'S RECORDED VOICE):
"QUI SEDES AD DEXTRAM PATRIS. *MISERERE NOBIS.* "

T. S. ELIOT:
My father? My biological father? *Have mercy*, indeed.

> (ELIOT fidgets in the shadows. Lights return.)

T. S. ELIOT(CONT'D):
Henry Ware Eliot--*my father who Waren't in heaven.* His ancestor, Andrew Eliot served the good Lord and the right honorable Samuel Farris at the Salem Witch trials. He poured the colored stones of carnality, corruption & shame into the crucible of the *Malleus Male Ficarum*—nineteen of the unclean were hanged ...

> (Sound of a body dropping through the gallows.)

T. S. ELIOT (CONT'D):
The Eliots were preternaturally disposed to the unnaturalness of nature. To me, father turned a deaf ear. He was scarred by scarlet fever - stone deaf from my earliest recollection. My mother?

(ELIOT sighs. He picks up the whip left
by VIVIENNE in the earlier scene.)

T. S. ELIOT (CONT'D):
Mother was descended from General Thomas Blood. "Blood!" It
was fated that Vivienne's menstrual cycle would be inordinate in its
flow. This whip is from the General's livery - mother was proficient
in its use: "Is this the hat I wish, a hat of red? If so let it be the
crown of martyrdom upon my head ..."

(ELIOT cracks the whip.)

T. S. ELIOT (CONT'D):
That's from her play, *Savonarola.* A vanity that, like its subject, was
committed to God's flame. Sorry mother. I love you more than I
can say or have ever said. "Life hath dealt kindly with me, yet men
know on earth no comfort like a mother's love." No, actually that
was Sophocles, *Oedipus The King* - the *Murray* translation ...

(ELIOT turns upstage and dons a black
mask (Jolson) or downstage & smears ash
into a black cross (Lent) upon his forehead.)

MUSIC CUE: *MY MAMMY.*)

T. S. ELIOT (SINGING):
Who cares if my friends are gone/
You'll find me holding on /
'Cause I can cling to my Mammy/
Who cares if my daddy shouts /
I'm nothing to rave about /
I'm everything to my mammy."

T. S. ELIOT (SINGING CONT'D):
The Sun Shines East, The Sun Shines West.)
I'm a coming, I hope I didn't make you wait /
I'm a coming, God I hope I'm not too late./
Mammy don't you know me? /It's your baby boy /
It's your lambie pie! I I'd walk a million miles /
For one of your smiles / My mamm-am-my…

ELIOT concludes on "Jolson knees" with outstretched arms. Scrim down. **DARKNESS.**)

**FROM THE DARKNESS
A TITLE CARD EMERGES
ON THE PROSCENIUM SCRIM:**

**II
THE GAME OF CHESS**

SCENE 7: THE 22ND DAY

Scrim Up. Lights up on ELIOT. He struggles to arise from the bent knee of his earlier position. He blocks THE MAN FROM LLOYDS from assisting him. He winces in pain. He rubs a sore knee.

T. S. ELIOT (TO MAN FROM LLOYDS):
No, no. Mother's little Tommy can stand his share of pain.

(Sound of cracking whip!)

T. S. ELIOT (CONT'D TO MAN FROM LLOYDS):
I often think of Mother in the waning light of day. My coat? No, I seem to have misplaced it. Yes, at my age I should be properly bundled. Thank you for your concern. My blood's beginning to thin as quickly as my hair. *It's time to turn back and mount the stair.* (LS) *Time to dissolve the floors of memory - its divisions and precisions.* (R) *Let us go then, you and I, when the evening is spread out against the sky like a patient etherized upon a table.*(LS)

(ELIOT peers and gestures to the Rear Screen.
A picture of two children dressed for winter, appears.)

T. S. ELIOT (CONT'D TO MAN FROM LLOYDS):
That's Vivienne and her cousin, *looking into the heart of light, the silence.*

(FADE REAR SCREEN.)

48

T. S. ELIOT (CONT'D):
She is frightened of the sled-slope but her cousin reassures her, *he said:*
(13, 14, 15, 41)

ACTOR D (VO):
Marie, Marie, hold on tight... (16)

T. S. ELIOT (TO MAN FROM LLOYDS):
and down they went... In the mountains, there you feel free. (16, 17, 18) *Let us go, through certain half-deserted streets, the muttering retreats of restless nights in one-night cheap hotels and sawdust restaurants with oyster-shells.* (LS)

> (MAURICE HAIGH-WOOD'S photo is briefly projected on the Rear Scrim. He is dressed in the military fatigues of a lower echelon officer, [ref. appendix] Lights up in a hotel bar. ACTOR C sits alone. ELIOT enters. He walks behind the bar with the full authority of a bartender. He polishes the bar-top and continues his monologue.)

T. S. ELIOT {TO MAN FROM LLOYDS):
This gentleman, as you see, is my brother-in-law, Maurice Haigh-Wood. He's trying to drown a memory that neither he nor I have successfully disowned. We both plotted Vivienne's commitment. Some of the papers have been conveniently misplaced, though Maurice often sees them smiling from the bottom of a snifter.

VIVIENNE HAIGH-WOOD (VO):
Moe, you little shit - say goodnight before you nip…

MAURICE HAIGH-WOOD (DRUNK):
Goonight, Bill. Goonight, Lou. (170)

T. S. ELIOT (TO MAN FROM LLOYDS):
And indeed there will be time to meet the faces you will meet… (LS)

> (A picture of Marilyn Monroe is projected on the Rear Screen. ACTOR B enters. She wears a Marilyn Monroe mask. MAURICE salutes her:)

MAURICE HAIGH-WOOD:
Goonight, *Norma* — Goonight, *Jean.*

> (A photo of JFK is projected on REAR SCREEN.
> Lights up in a bedroom of the ruins. ACTOR D
> enters. He wears a JFK mask. He fondles ACTOR
> B's Marilyn. He removes her mask. It is
> VIVIENNE. She removes his mask. It is
> BERTRAND RUSSELL.

> *BERTIE* places a bracelet on *VIVI'S* bare arm -
> he kisses and licks her arm to the nape of her neck
> and then forces her to the floor.)

MAURICE HAIGH-WOOD (CONT' D):
Goonight, Ta Ta. [170,171]

DARKNESS

FROM THE DARKNESS
A TITLE CARD EMERGES
ON THE PROSCENIUM SCRIM:

III
THE FIRE SERMON

T. S. ELIOT (VO TO MAN FROM LLOYDS):
*And I have known the arms already, known them all - Arms that
are braceleted and bare* [LS] ... Jack and his Marilyn *Magdalene*
will soon be in your lair ...

(LIGHTS UP on ELIOT.)

T. S. ELIOT (CONT'D TO MAN FROM LLOYDS):
Russell tired of his conquest. He went on to younger game. But I
stayed on beyond my humanity and shame. I did all I could for her.

(MORE)

T. S. ELIOT (CONT'D)
She had to have constant medication and psychiatric care. My health deteriorated along with hers. My "voices" roared through the remainder of the *Twenties*. On the pretense of Sabbatical, I left her in the fall of '32 - it was finished! She wandered London like a *shivering restless painted shadow.*[FR]

(A ghostly photo of VIVIENNE
is projected on the Rear Screen.)

T. S. ELIOT (CONT'D):
I often fled before the darkness of her shade. We never divorced. She was a broken widow longing for a face she'd never find within a window. The widows of November? Jackie or Marina?

(JACKIE KENNEDY & MARINA
OSWALD'S photos, [ref. APPENDIX], replace
VIVIENNE'S photo on the Rear Screen.

T. S. ELIOT (CONT'D):
A Knight, of crystal purity, is the only hope of healing in a Wasteland.

(Dissolve the widows' photos.)

MUSIC CUE: Theme, "Sailor's Lament" -
Wagner's *Tristan Und Isolde:*)

SAILOR (SINGING VO):
Frisch weht der Wind [31] *Der Heimat zu.*[32]

T. S. ELIOT (CONT'D):
Jackie gave me a chess piece at Arlington ...

MAN FROM LLOYDS (ELIOT'S VO, DISTANTLY):
"CRUCIFIXUS ETIAM, ET SEPULTUS EST."

T. S. ELIOT:
"HE WAS CRUCIFIED FOR US AND WAS BURIED."
Yes, the set belonged to Jack.

>(Project Memorial Portrait of JFK –
>APPENDIX).

SAILOR (SINGING VO):
Mein Irisch Kind, [33] *Wo weilest du?* [34]

T. S. ELIOT (CONT'D TO MAN FROM LLOYDS):
Marina's service for her husband, Lee, was a less illustrious affair.

T. S. ELIOT (CONT'D):
She removed her wedding band and placed it on her husband's hand - a reversal of that detail so poignant in the Wagner. Yes - yes, you're quite right - there was a third widow lost among the fated carnage. A policeman's wife. Officer (PAUSE) Officer Tippit's widow. Strangely, her name was Marie. Marie, (PAUSE) my Mary Magdalene, and my lost Marina ...

>(The Memorial Portrait of Kennedy is replaced by
>the trio of Marie Tippit, Marina Oswald, and
>Jacqueline Kennedy.) [APPENDIX]

>**MUSIC CUE:** Gotterdammerung Act 3,
>Scene 1. The three Rhinemaidens' song is heard
>and continues behind ELIOT'S next lines.)

CHORUS (EMI RECORDING):
Weialala leia Wallala leialala, Weialala leia Wallalaleialala. [276,277,290,291]

T. S. ELIOT (TO MAN FROM LLOYDS):
I have heard the mermaids sing each to each. I do not think they will sing to me ...

T. S. ELIOT (CONT'D):
We have lingered by sea girls wreathed with seaweed red & brown ...

>(The Rhinemaidens go silent.)

T. S. ELIOT (CONT'D):
till human voices wake us and we drown . . . (LS)

(**DARKNESS**. VIVIENNE'S shrill voice
follows immediately from the dark.)

VIVIENNE HAIGH-WOOD (VO):
*I can't help it - it's those pills I took to bring it off. The chemist said it would be
alright but I've never been the same.* (158, 159, 161)

(Lights up on VIVIENNE. She sits alone on
stone bench in the center of the ruins. ELIOT
enters.)

T. S. ELIOT:
You are a proper fool . . . (162)

VIVIENNE HAIGH- WOOD:
What you get married for if you didn't want to have children! (164) Bertie
would've had 'em. He's a Yorkshire lad. He likes the pudding as
well as the pie!

(Lights down on VIVIENNE. She mutters mutely
in the shadows. ELIOT walks behind her to a
bureau drawer.)

T. S. ELIOT (TO MAN FROM LLOYDS):

(ELIOT removes Princip's pistol from the
drawer. He unscrews and removes the silencer
tube from the barrel of the gun.)

T. S. ELIOT (TO MAN FROM LLOYDS):
For Vivienne Haigh-Wood Eliot and the jaunty JFK ...

(MORE)

(ELIOT puts the gun to the back of VIVIENNE'S head. She stops her silent muttering.)

T. S. ELIOT (TO MAN FROM LLOYDS):
Each knew their last tomorrow ...

VIVIENNE HAIGH-WOOD (EXCITEDLY):
He likes the pudding as well as the pie!

T. S. ELIOT (CONT'D):
... on the twenty-second day!

(ELIOT fires a shot to VIVIENNE'S head.
She crumples to the floor.
He stands menacingly over her body.)

DATE STAMP:
JANUARY 22, 1947
NORTHUMBERLAND HOUSE ASYLUM

(He fires a second shot to her abdomen. The final shot is a deafening concussion. Quick Spot on ACTOR C. He raises a glass of ELIOT'S favorite *Single Malt*.)

MAURICE HAIGH-WOOD:
Goonight, Viv. *Goonight.* [171]

DARKNESS

END OF ACT I

ACT II

A solo flute begins an arrangement of *Swing Low Sweet Chariot.* **The orchestral arrangement continues with** *Quarter to Nine/You Made Me Love You* **and concludes with a raucously good humored and orchestral** *Toot, Toot, Tootsie Goodbye.* **The curtain opens to the Doric ruin of Eliot's childhood home. ELIOT lights a Gauloises. The poet takes an expansive puff from the glowing cigarette. He coughs and struggles to catch his breath...**

SCENE 1: THE OLD DICTUM

T. S. ELIOT (TO MAN FROM LLOYDS):
Killing me? Perhaps. *Dies Irae:* The heart stops. *Dies Illa:* Oxygen fails the brain. *Solvent saeclum in favilla:* Earth and ass are turned to ash. There's little difference between death with Anglican aid or death while riding in a motorcade. What is the old dictum?

> "A man can surely do what he wishes to do
> but he cannot determine what he wishes."

I tried to control the disparate voices they split me asunder. Their chaotic din was the cacophony of sin ...

> (Enter VIVIENNE. She speaks facing
> the audience - an embodied memory.)

VIVIENNE HAIGH-WOOD:
My nerves are bad tonight. Yes bad![111] Tom, I need a weekend by the sea ...

> **MUSIC CUE**: *Gotterdamerung* Act 3 Scene 1. The
> Rhinemaidens' Theme is interfused with a fugue
> of conflicting voices. It is played behind the
> dialogue and enters in more fully as indicated.)

RHINEMAIDEDNS (RECORDED VO):
Weialala leia Wallala leialala . . . (276, 277)

> (MAURICE, [ACTOR C]; and RUSSELL, [ACTOR D]; join VIVIENNE, ACTOR B]. They surround ELIOT, [ACTOR A] with their "chaotic din" spoken out to the audience:)

BERTRAND RUSSELL:
Here we have it - the key to Tourquay.

VIVIENNE HAIGH-WOOD:
Is it proper, Tom? I'll be alone with him for half the holiday.

T. S. ELIOT:
He's a trusted friend on whom we do depend.

BERTRAND RUSSELL (ASIDE TO AUDIENCE):
By the *sea* beneath a cliff,
I'll do her in a rented skiff!

RHINEMAIDENS (RECORDED VO):
Weilala leia... allalala (290)

VIVIENNE HAIGH-WOOD:
Highbury bore me. Richmond and Kew undid me. For Richmond I raised my knees supine on the floor of his *narrow canoe...* (294,295)

BERTRAND RUSSELL:
What's a little blood between friends?

MAURICE HAIGH-WOOD (ACTOR C):
Goonight, Bertie.

RHINEMAIDENDS (RECORDED VO):
Wallala leialala (291)

T. S. ELIOT:
I came upon the sylvan scene~ the change of Philomel, by the barbarous king, so rudely forced. (99)

VIVIENNE HAIGH-WOOD:
After the event he wept. He promised "a new start." I made no comment. What should I resent? (297,298,299)

MAURICE HAIGH-WOOD (ACTOR C):
Goonight, Viv.

RHINEMAIDENDS (RECORDED VO):
Wallala leialala (291)

BERTRAND RUSSELL:
Please, Tom - use the flat at your leisure. I'll see your wife at her pleasure.

T. S. ELIOT:
and still she cried: (103)

VIVIENNE HAIGH-WOOD:
What are you thinking of? What thinking? What? I never know what you are thinking. (113,114)

RHINEMAIDENS (RECORDED VO):
Weialala leia (277)

T. S. ELIOT:
I think we are in rat's alley where the dead men lost their bones. (115,116)

MAURICE HAIGH-WOOD:
Goonight, Tom. He's a good man, Viv.

VIVIENNE HAIGH-WOOD:
He's a good man, Maurice. *Goonight,* Tom.

BERTRAND RUSSELL:
He's a fine lad. Top of his class. Hats off, hats off to Thomas Stearns Eliot!

(ACTORS, B,C & D jeer and cheer the despondent poet.)

MAURICE HAIGH-WOOD:
Goonight!

T. S. ELIOT:
Noooooooooooooooooooooo. Stop time! Stop ... stop

(He collapses to the floor. The Rhinemaidens stop singing.)

T. S. ELIOT (IN A SHATTERED WHISPER):
Time to stop ...

SCENE 2: THE EUMENIDES

DARKNESS. A sobbing is heard in the dark. **LIGHTS SLOWLY UP..** ELIOT is alone on the stage. He looks about in a private terror. His mind becomes increasingly unhinged in his confession to THE MAN FROM LLOYDS.

T. S. ELIOT (TO MAN FROM LLOYDS):
What place is this? What quarter of the world?[M] The Russell affair? (COUGHS) Yes, there was pain enough to be enjoyed by all. Bertie was a wolf, indeed, but the wolf in bed with "Little Red" was my private *letch* and wretched scheme! Ha! Ha! Now there's a tale as grim as any found in Grimm or in God's "Good Book," grey and grand! Russell was a god and "Mary" was his maid - but my Vivi was no virgin, no Catholic should complain. I put the two of them together - we made a trinity of sin. They fell deep into perdition because I pushed them in! Ha! Ha!

(WE HEAR THE **HOWLING OF THE HELLHOUNDS**. ELIOT looks furtively about in increasing dementia.)

T. S. ELIOT:
Listen ... listen to my pretties. *You don't see them, you don't* – but there's no rest from them. The Eumenides are always close at hand or hem. Heel, ladies! Bastards all—Listen ... You can hear their fervent scratching ... Take heed, take heed - the bitches mount the wall!

> Loud growling and barking on the sound system. ELIOT falls to his knees and puts his hands above his head as if trying to expel the imminent attack of the leaping hellhounds.)

T. S. ELIOT:
OWWWWWWWWWWWWWWWWWWWWWWWWEEEEEEE EEEEEEEEEEEEEEEEE!

DARKNESS

SCENE 3: PAOLO AND FRANCESCA

> A wind begins to rise on the sound system. Lighting changes to the deep ochre of a flame. We enter the "Inferno" of ELIOT'S imagination.
>
> On the Rear Screen a projected title card reads:
>
> THE 2ND CIRCLE.
>
> SPOT on VIVIENNE in an evening gown at stage left. She holds a book in one hand, at her side.
>
> The RUSSELL picture is projected on the Rear Screen. A wolf snout has been crudely drawn on RUSSELL'S face. The wind increases.

SPOT on **LORD RUSSELL, ACTOR D** in wolf-mask, coat-tails and exaggerated wolf-claws. He poses with top hat in hand. **LORD RUSSELL** puts on his top hat. He extends his hand to **VIVIENNE. VIVIENNE** drops her book. Enter **ELIOT. VIVIENNE** and **RUSSELL** begin their dance at about *a quarter to nine:*

MUSIC CUE: *ABOUT A QUARTER TO NINE/ YOU MADE ME LOVE YOU*

T. S. ELIOT (SINGING):
Life begins when somebody's eyes look into your own
Life begins when you get your gal all alone
From morning until twilight, I don't know I'm alive
But I know, love begins at 8:45

(ELIOT taps RUSSELL & takes VIVIENNE)

BERTRAND RUSSELL (SINGING):
Give me, Give me, what I cry for.
You know you've got the brand of kisses that I'd die for.
You know you've made me love you.

(VIVIENNE abandons ELIOT. RUSSELL and VIVIENNE dance intimately at Stage Right.)

T. S. ELIOT (SINGING):
The stars are gonna twinkle and shine
This evening about a quarter to nine
Her lovin' arms (her lovin' arms)
Are gonna tenderly twine (are gonna tenderly twine)
Around me, around a quarter to nine...

ELIOT shoots LORD RUSSELL in a loud "rat-ta-tat" blast of "bullets" from his cane. SPATTERS of BLOOD are PROJECTED "in time" with the concussions...

VIVIENNE looks on in horror as RUSSELL is violently riddled with the imaginary ammunition. He falls to the floor. VIVIENNE kneels next to his lifeless body. Lights down. ELIOT walks to the front of the stage. Scrim Down.)

T. S. ELIOT (TO MAN FROM LLOYDS):
Yes, Yes. Of course, Bertrand Arthur William Russell, 3rd Earl Russell of Kingston Russell is still very much alive in 1965 – the lovely succubus, of course, is dead nearing two decades now, but that damn satyr will survive us all! During the war, *"it"* supplied us with a stipend that I was desperate to decline. We were the *Moderns*--with flesh corrupting on the battlefields the press of living flesh was not to be denied.

LIGHTS DOWN

SCENE 4: THE VIOLET HOUR

Lights up slowly, through the scrim. The photo of the ruined cityscape returns to the Rear Screen. The frozen sunlight casts an eerie glow on the Doric Temple. VIVIENNE stands alone at Center Stage. She calls out to ELIOT from the ruins of a Wasteland.

VIVIENNE HAIGH-WOOD:
Tom, are you there? I don't care much, for being alone down here.

(Up Scrim. ELIOT joins his first wife. He leads her to a bench. They sit and he cradles her in his arms.)

T. S. ELIOT:
Yes, Viv. You're not alone.

VIVIENNE HAIGH-WOOD:
I heard you talking to Maurice. And then it came to me: You are the voice in the fog. You are the whisper of midnight and memory.

T. S. ELIOT:
And you're not afraid?

VIVIENNE HAIGH-WOOD:
I was at first. I thought you were a ghost - so I turned my head askance.

(ELIOT comforts her as if she were a child.)

T. S. ELIOT:
That's the way of ghosts. We finally face only them if by fleeting chance.

(VIVIENNE stands, suspicious of the intimacy.)

VIVIENNE HAIGH-WOOD:
 Is that why I'm on the fade, Tom?

T. S. ELIOT:
To clean from the mind the illusion of... light. (CP)
We fade from light to shade as we seek illumination.

VIVIENNE HAIGH-WOOD:
You always said you loved *me and you kept on saying you were in love. You had cause to love me. I entered you in my heart.* (WLB) I believe you were trying to persuade yourself that you had entered me in yours. *I wonder now how you could have thought you were in love with me.* (CP)

T. S. ELIOT:
Everybody told me that I was and then *they told me how well suited we were.* (CP)

VIVIENNE HAIGH-WOOD:
Your friends had little use for me and overuse for you. *It's a pity you had no opinion of your own.*[CP] *The ivory men made company between us.* [WLE] I'm sorry for you, Tom—*bloody peeping Tommy* ...

VIVIENNE HAIGH-WOOD (CONT'D):
How much longer do I have?

T. S. ELIOT:
It's time.

VIVIENNE HAIGH-WOOD:
I'm chilled to the bone.

T. S. ELIOT:
Time.

VIVIENNE HAIGH-WOOD (VO):
Tom, the answers don't much matter when you let the questions go.

T. S. ELIOT (VO):
At the violet hour letting them go is often answer enough ... [220]

VIVIENNE HAIGH-WOOD:
Goodnight, Tom. I don't need a shove - The North Star shall be my beacon...

(VIV smiles at her former husband. She exits *under the brown fog of a winter's* dawn. [208]

MUSIC CUE: ELIOT begins singing/speaking a modified cover of: *SWING LOW, SWEET CHARIOT.*

T. S. ELIOT (SING/SPEAK):
Swing low, sweet chariot. Coming for to carry me home. Swing low, sweet chariot. Coming for to carry me home ...

PROJECT DATE STAMP & SLIDES BEHIND SINGING:

NOVEMBER 22, 1963 - LOVE FIELD

(Slides of Kennedy's coffin ascending a conveyor belt to Air Force One are projected slowly on the Rear Screen. The coffin disappears into the airplane. The song's 2nd verse is comingled with the Catholic nursery rhyme: *Mary, Mary, Quite Contrary*, sung to the same melody.)

T. S. ELIOT (SING/SPEAK):
Swing low, sweet chariot. How does your garden grow?
　　Swing low, sweet chariot. With silver bells and cockle shells
　　　　Sing cuckolds all in a row...

T. S. ELIOT (TO MAN FROM LLOYDS):
Good night, *My Mary, Mary, Quite Contrary: Et in Unum Dominum Jesum Christum.*(LT6)　I believe in one Lord, Jesus Christ , *Sleep in Peace,* John Fitzgerald Fisher King: *Kyrie Eleison, requiescant in pace—*

(The JFK Memorial Portrait is projected on the Rear Screen.)

T. S. ELIOT (CONT'D):
Jack's a good Irish lad. His creed won't desert him now: *Sedet ad dexteram Dei Patris—he sits at the right hand of the Father.* God's speed, my liege and late-lamented sovereign.

DARKNESS. The roar of the departing Air Force One fills the theater.

SILENCE.

MUSIC CUE: ELIOT sings final refrain in

DARKNESS

T. S. ELIOT (SPEAKING IN THE DARKNESS):
Coming for to carry me home...

**FROM THE DARKNESS
A TITLE CARD EMERGES
ON THE PROSCENIUM SCRIM:**

IV

DEATH BY WATER

FADE TITLE. UP SCRIM.

SCENE 5: EAST COKER

**ELIOT sits alone at a table. He begins to lay
out the cards of a Tarot deck.**

T. S. ELIOT (TO THE MAN FROM LLOYDS):
My mother! Charlotte, taught me what I know of Tarot. In her the
Christian and the Pagan were formidably combined. I was doubled
from the start!

(ELIOT transitions into WILD CAT
COLOMBO. The voice of Walter
Cronkite is heard in VO.)

WALTER CRONKITE (VO):
Thirty minutes after the murder of officer J.D. Tippit -Lee Harvey
Oswald was apprehended in the Texas Theater.

(SPOT on RUSSELL/OSWALD sitting in **AN
AISLE SEAT IN THE LIVE THEATER
AUDIENCE.** He is in his perennial top and tails.
ELIOT, as WILD CAT COLOMBO, continues his
revenge fantasy. He runs down to the edge of the
stage.)

WILD CAT/ELIOT (POINTING):
There he is ... that's our boy!

(RUSSELL stands. He is blinded by the spot light. ACTOR C, dressed as a Dallas cop, wrestles RUSSELL to the aisle floor and whacks him unconscious with a baton. **SPOT OFF. DARKNESS.**)

LOCATION STAMP:
MISSOURI RIVER - ST. LOUIS

(Lights slowly up on several gravestones in a corner of the ruins. VIVIENNE'S Grecian Urn, inscribed with a white rose, sits next to the gravestones. ELIOT is heard in Voice Over.)

T. S. ELIOT (VO TO MAN FROM LLOYDS):
I was born on that bluff overlooking the river - the seventh of seven born to Henry Ware Eliot and Charlotte Stearns. These roses were shipped from East Coker at Somerset, where they served the *Royals* down the centuries and graced many a soldier's grave. Perhaps…

(PAUSE.Enter ELIOT)

T. S. ELIOT:
…even one whose *bones were mixed in the mud of Gallipoli.* It is sunset at the Luxenbourg Gardens. Jean crosses the court yard with Lilacs in his arms ⋯

T. S. ELIOT (SPEAKING TO AN UNSUNG MELDOY):
Fresh blows the wind.

T. S. ELIOT:
To the homeland …

T. S. ELIOT:
My Irish Child,

T. S. ELIOT:
Where will I find you?

T. S. ELIOT(CONT'D TO MAN FROM LLOYDS):
These smaller flowers are for the still-born who never knew a rose's scent or bloom. White roses for the lassies, Red roses for the lads. *"Tu se' ombra vedi. Puoi, la quantitate: "for thou art a shade and a shade thou seest."*

(Enter VIVIENNE.)

VIVIENNE HAIGH-WOOD:
They called me the hyacinth girl. (36)

T. S. ELIOT:
It's your line, Viv. I wouldn't let Ezra strike it from the text.

VIVIENNE HAIGH-WOOD:
No, Tom. It was your line, your line for Jean - *"mort aux Dardanelles." You do not know what life is - you who hold it in your hands.* (Portrait) Memory of loss is the most impossible of rivals. But I was in for the penny, in for *Mr. Pound.* Only now, Tom - do I feel, at last, on equal footing.

T. S. ELIOT:
And the North Star shall betoken ...

VIVIENNE HAIGH-WOOD:
the cloistered rose of East Coker.

> (ELIOT hands her the urn. She walks to the river's edge and begins to disperse her own ashes.)

VIVIENNE HAIGH-WOOD (CONT'D):
Sweet Thames, run softly til I end my song. (183)

T. S. ELIOT:
Sweet Thames, run softly, for I speak not loud or long. (164)

DARKNESS

67

SCENE 6: THE HANGED MAN OF CANTERBURY

Lights slowly up. The shadow of THE MAN FROM LLOYDS appears projected on the Proscenium Scrim within Canterbury Cathedral.

MAN FROM LLOYDS (ELIOT'S RECORDED VOICE):
The conspirators spilled Thomas Becket's brains upon a crypt below the blessed floor of Canterbury. *I do not find the hanged man* [54, 55] *but I saw with my own eyes the Sibyl of Cumae hanging in a jar...* [WLEP] and then I heard a godless shuffle overhead beneath the vaulted bars...

> Through the scrim we hear and see a body dropping from the fabled ceiling. We spy the body of a hanged man dangling from a rope and obscured by shadow. It is lowered to the floor. BERTRAND RUSSELL (in top hat) and MAURICE HAIGH-WOOD (in officer's cap), remove the rope from the hanged man's neck. They carry the body to a lounge chair. They exit. The hanged man sits up. He is T.S. Eliot.

MAN FROM LLOYDS (ELIOT'S RECORDED VOICE):
And then the boys said to her: "Sibyl, what do you want?" [WLEP]

T.S. ELIOT:
She replied: "I want to die..." [WLEP]

> ELIOT begins to apply the makeup he often wore when pursuing his degradation in the London night.

MAN FROM LLOYDS (ELIOT'S RECORDED VOICE):
Yes, Mr. Eliot, let's add a little color to the cheek. *There will be time to meet the faces that you meet, there will be time to murder and create,* [LS] we wouldn't want our martyred saint to think thee weak...

> Eliot applies the **green, orange & red colors of the HERON PORTRAIT** (appendix), now fading in on the Rear Scrim. The poet's face suggests a harlequin or a vampire. The poet is applying his **DEATH MASK**.

MAN FROM LLOYDS (ELIOT'S RECORDED VOICE):
The whipping tail is not more still then when I smell a blooded-banker *dangling from a friendly tree...*(LOM)

> (The Shadow of THE MAN FROM LLOYDS cracks General Blood's whip on the Proscenium Scrim. ELIOT falls to his knees in a direness of fear and supplication.)

T. S. ELIOT:
The sin of the world is upon our head. The agony of the saints is upon our head. (MC)

> (THE MAN FROM LLOYDS, as the *WHIP-MASTER* of this Act, cuts closer to the bone than he did as the *ELECTRO-THERAPIST* of Act I.)

MAN FROM LLOYDS (ELIOT'S RECORDED VOICE):
Now, Mr. Eliot. No more *fiddle* and no more *faddle*. Let's to the brass tacks of it, shall we?

You used the woman. She helped you with the poem - she helped you with the journal. And then you used "Bertie" to use the woman for whom you had no use. You used the Mathematician to subtract Ophelia from your life.

T. S. ELIOT:
As you've divined: Services rendered, payment applied - portrait of a twist and the twisted pimping of her poet-prince.

> (Sound of cracking whip! ELIOT jolts from the imagined lash. He falls forward.)

T. S. ELIOT (CONT'D):
Lord have mercy on us. (MC)

MAN FROM LLOYDS (ELIOT'S RECORDED VOICE):
Yes, Mr. Eliot, I'll note the request. It says here that :*"You tossed a blanket from the bed. You dozed and watched the night reveal the thousand sordid images of which your soul was constituted."* (P) I trust that's a fair reading of a lecher's *lech*?

T. S. ELIOT (CONT'D):
You've done your homework! Yes - *Birth, copulation and death.* (SWA)
I begrudged the first, forsook the second and I deny the third!

(Sound of cracking whip! ELIOT writhes in agony.)

T. S. ELIOT (CONT'D):
Christ have mercy on us. (MC)

(**MUSIC CUE**: Theme, Sailor's Lament" -
Wagner's *Tristan Und Isolde.* The picture of Jean
Verdenal replaces the Heron Portrait, on the Rear
Screen.)

SAILOR (SINGING VO):
Mein Irisch Kind ... (33)

MAN FROM LLOYDS (ELIOT'S RECORDED VOICE):
Yes, the beauty of the boy would not be well enjoyed if he found
his famed *Tiresias,* at best ...

SAILOR (SINGING VO):
Wo weilest du? (34)

MAN FROM LLOYDS (ELIOT'S RECORDED VOICE)
-an old man with wrinkled female breasts! (219)

T. S. ELIOT:
Nooooooooooooooooooooooooooooooooooooooooooooooooooo
oooo!

(Sound of cracking whip! ELIOT is laid flat —
A broken, old man.)

T. S. ELIOT (WEEPING, QUIETLY):
Please, please - no.

(Fade photo of Jean Verdenal)

MAN FROM LLOYDS (ELIOT'S RECORDED VOICE):
Wipe your hand across your face and laugh: (P) You and Maurice made a jolly pair, dividing dividends between you as if presumptive heirs.

Your *worlds revolved like ancient women gathering fuel in vacant lots* (P) above her bones. Neither of you bothered to correct the dates you carved upon her stone.

T. S. ELIOT:
I didn't kill her! The dead should find their own way.
How much longer will she stay? Why do I find her here?

MAN FROM LLOYDS (ELIOT'S RECORDED VOICE):
This *is where one sees them - the last apparent refuge, the safe shelter. That is the way of Spectres.* (FR)

You always treated her as a child. In Paris, among the lost, you acknowledged her last. She died of heart failure, eighteen years ago, come the 22nd day…

(Sound of gunshot.)

MAN FROM LLOYDS (ELIOT'S RECORDED VOICE):
It was as much your failure of heart, as hers.

MAN FROM LLOYDS (ELIOT'S RECORDED VOICE):
Was it worth it, Mr. Eliot?

We wouldn't want a woman's nerves to interrupt the adulation the world.

The literati will come to *see the moment of your greatness flicker—*
the eternal Footman hold your coat and snicker. (LS)

What remains when few remember and none are left to cheer?

(Sound of cracking whip!)

71

T. S. ELIOT:
OWWWWWWWWWWWWWWWWWWWWWWWWWWWWEE
EEEEEEEEEEEEEEEEEEEEEEEEEEEE!

(The wind begins to rise. Eliot clutches at his coat.
He looks furtively and futilely to the left and right.)

T. S. ELIOT (CONT'D IN A WHISPER):
I am *an old man, a dull head among windy spaces* (G) ...

DARKNESS

FLASH OF LIGHTNING

THE WIND INCREASES

PEAL OF THUNDER

FLASH OF LIGHTNING

DARKNESS

FROM THE DARKNESS
A TITLE CARD EMERGES
ON THE PROSCENIUM SCRIM:

V
<u>WHAT THE THUNDER SAID</u>

Replace title card with a rolling peal of thunder and the caption:

THE 7TH CIRCLE

SCENE 7: THE 7TH CIRCLE

On the rear scrim: **STOCK NEWSREEL FOOTAGE** of President Kennedy's arrival at Love Field, Dallas-- November 1963. Jack & Jackie *deboard* and descend to the waiting limousine. **NEWSREEL OFF. SPOT ON ELIOT—STAGE LEFT.** He wears a bowler hat and carries his signature umbrella. His **GREEN, ORANGE & RED** makeup accentuates a mad gleam in his eyes. He has become *THE MAN FROM LLOYDS*—he has become *DEATH...*

DATE STAMP:
12:25 P.M. NOVEMBER 22, 1963
DALLAS TEXAS

SPOT ON ACTOR C wearing a JFK mask, sitting with **VIVIENNE** on the third bench of a "Limousine", (as in the Act I Archduke Assassination), at Stage Right.

ELIOT IMAGINES that he is on the 6th floor of the Texas School Book Depository - recreated in the 7th Circle of his private Hell.

Replace Date Stamp with a caption that reads:

THE 6TH FLOOR

73

Jack and Jacqueline Kennedy wave in a SLOW-MOTION MIME from the third bench of their "limo". ELIOT speaks to the audience. His voice is measured and implacable.

T. S. ELIOT:
So many waiting, how many waiting? What did it matter on such a day. Only there is shadow under this red rock ... (24~25)

WALTER CRONKITE (VO):
The Dallas police department has been augmented by 400 off-duty officers...

T. S. ELIOT (CONT'D):
Come in under the shadow of this red rock. And I will show something different than your shadow at morning striding behind you and your shadow at evening striding to meet you ... (26-29)

WALTER CRONKITE (VO):
There has been concern that demonstrations might...

T. S. ELIOT (CONT'D):
I will show you fear ... (30)

(Jackie whispers to the President. They both laugh..)

T. S. ELIOT (CONT'D):
in a handfull of dust. (30)

(BERTRAND RUSSELL (as Oswald) enters in top hat and tails. He carries a rifle in both hands. He bows as if offering a sacred relic. .ELIOT takes the proffered rifle. RUSSELL exits.)

WALTER CRONKITE (VO):
... embarrass the President.

T. S. ELIOT (CONT'D):
Greater care we'd take of the choices that we make if we saw them on the dark side of forever...

(ELIOT aims into the audience. **LIGHTING TURNS GREEN. HE FIRES THE FIRST SHOT. ACTOR C (JFK) mimes being hit—FREEZE FRAME.**)

T. S. ELIOT (CONT'D):
Death has a hundred hands and walks by a thousand ways. (MC)

The **LIGHTING TURNS ORANGE.**

(**ELIOT FIRES THE SECOND SHOT.**
The concussion increases in volume.
Kennedy lurches to the right, his head
slamming into the side door—**FREEZE FRAME.**)

T. S. ELIOT (CONT' D):
He *may come in the sight of all, he may pass unseen unheard.*
Come whispering in the ear, or to a sudden shock to the skull ... (MC)

(The **LIGHTING TURNS RED.**
ELIOT FIRES THE THIRD SHOT.
It is a deafening concussion. VIVIENNE
grabs both sides of her "husband's"
head—**FREEZE FRAME.**)

(**FADE THE ASSASSINATION TO DARK.**)

(RUSSELL returns. ELIOT gives him the rifle.
RUSSELL exits. ELIOT notes the time.)

T. S. ELIOT (CONT'D):
The President will be pronounced dead in thirty-eight minutes…

WALTER CRONKITE:
From Dallas Texas, *the flash,* apparently official. President
Kennedy died at 1:00 P.M. – Central Standard Time--thirty-eight
minutes ago…"

T.S. ELIOT:
It is a mere formality. *He who was living is now dead.*
We who were living are now dying—with a little patience. (320,329,330)

T. S. ELIOT (CONT'D, AFTER A PAUSE):
Who then shall plead for me? Who will intercede for me in my most need? (MC)
After the torchlight red on sweaty faces, after the silence in the gardens, after the
agony in stony places... (322-327)   After it all, the assassin will be found to
have acted quite alone—but I awake each night to find the prints
upon his rifle—are decidedly my own—my little Vivi, Vivi was the
only one who made me glad—my Vivi Magdalene was the only one
who knew me mad ...

                   (ELIOT stands. He crooks his head.)

T. S. ELIOT (CONT'D):
So my little Mary, Mary quite contrary... to the madhouse *you* must go ...

       (Suddenly, his Anglican pretensions desert him.
       He speaks in a flat, mid-western accent.)

T. S. ELIOT (CONT'D):
I didn't have the courage to kill her--I buried her alive!

       (SPOT ON VIVIENNE & ELIOT. They address the
       audience as if in separate worlds of memory.)

VIVIENNE-HAIGH WOOD:
What is that noise? (117)

T. S. ELIOT:
The wind under the door. (118)

VIVIENNE HAIGH-WOOD:
What is that noise now? What is the wind doing? (119)

T. S. ELIOT:
Nothing again, nothing. (120)

VIVIENNE HAIGH-WOOD:
Do you know nothing? Do you see nothing? Do you remember nothing? (121,122)

T. S. ELIOT:

I remember, those are pearls that were his eyes. (123) Our friends believed the victim to be me and I was not disposed to disagree. "Poor Tom," they thought. *"Poor Tom's acold* and Viv's a witch, we'd all prefer he'd leave the bitch!"

VIVIENNE HAIGH-WOOD:

Falling towers, Jerusalem, Athens, London... Unreal. (374,375,376)

T.S. ELIOT:

O city, city (259) *- so many, I had not thought death had undone so many ...* (61,62,63)

CHORUS (FROM AFAR):

Goosey, Goosey, gander whither shall we wander?

VIVIENNE HAIGH-WOOD:

I love you, Tom. Through it all, I still love you.

> (ELIOT turns his back on his first wife. She gulps back a sob in measureless pain. He begins to walk away. She reaches after the only husband she has known. He stops. She lets her arm drop in resignation. She turns away, as well. VIVIENNE HAIGH-WOOD fades back into shadows.)

T. S. ELIOT (TO HIMSELF):

Upstairs, downstairs ... (PAUSE)

> (He appears to shrink in pain, decrepitude and shame.)

T. S. ELIOT (CONCLUDING):

in the fields you saunter ...

> (ELIOT stops abruptly. He begins to breathe heavily. He puts his hand to his chest and grimaces in pain.)

DARKNESS

CODA
DATE STAMP:
JANUARY 4, 1965 - LONDON

A coughing is heard on the sound system.
Lights slowly up among the ruins revealing a hospital bed with its white privacy curtains open. VALERIE, ACTOR B (in glasses), sits next to her husband, THOMAS STEARNS ELIOT.

T. S. ELIOT (CONT'D):
Thanks Val, I promise I'll only nap a minute…

VALERIE kisses her husband on the forehead. She encloses the white privacy curtains around him. SHE DEPARTS. SCRIM DOWN. DARKNESS. An EKG MONITOR shows the poet's heartbeat—the beat is heard prominently on the sound system. The wind begins to rise. A wolf-cry and peal of thunder is heard.

SHADOW PLAY: The PRIVACY ENCLOSURE STRETCHES & EXTENDS FROM THE FLOOR TO THE RAFTERS. It is lit brilliantly from within. THE MAN FROM LLOYDS appears as a GIGANTIC LOOMING SHADOW. He hovers over the bedridden poet with the electric pads of a DEFIBRILLATOR in each hand.

WILD CAT COLOMBO [ACTOR A] ENTERS. ELIOT'S "suppressed self" stands CENTER STAGE in front of the projected shadow of the dying poet. He holds his Stetson to his chest. The thunder intensifies as ELIOT'S failing heart struggles to beat on the lowered scrim and sound system.

BERTRAND RUSSELL:
Stretched out on the table you are a *piece of furniture in a repair shop* (CP)…

WILD CAT COLOMBO:
a broken settee—no carpenter, no nail…

VIVIENNE HAIGH-WOOD:
The fire within burns green... (95)

(The Shadow of THE MAN FROM LLOYDS applies the **FIRST JOLT** of the defibrillator pads on the projected shadow of the poet—the **LIGHTNING FLASHES GREEN.** ELIOT jolts upward... then falls back to the peal of thunder.)

MAURICE HAIGH-WOOD:
These fragments you *have shored against your ruin...* (MC)

WILD CAT COLOMBO:
Buck up little buckeroo... there must something in the kitty ...

(*WILD CAT* becomes pale and short of breath)

BERTRAND RUSSELL:
Shall I at least put your lands in order? (420)

WILD CAT COLOMBO:
Mon semblable, mon frère— (70) Sweet Jesus, Tommy—you're breaking my goddamn heart!

VIVIENNE HAIGH-WOOD:
... and orange, (95)

(*WILD CAT* falls to his knees in a paroxysm of pain. The shadow of THE MAN FROM LLOYDS applies the **SECOND JOLT—the LIGHTNING FLASHES ORANGE. T**hunder & heartbeat loudly reverberate.)

WILD CAT COLOMBO (AS IF A FRIGHTENED CHILD):
London bridge is falling down, falling down, falling down... (427)
London bridge is...Tommy? Tom-Tom my lad——Tommy me laddie...

MAURICE HAIGH-WOOD:
For those that surround you, the masked actors, **all there is of you is your** *body ...*(CP) ***And then...***

VIVIANNE HAIGH-WOOD:
...framed by the colored stones. [95]

(THE MAN FROM LLOYDS applies the **THIRD & FINAL JOLT**—the **LIGHTNING FLASHES RED.** WILD CAT COLOMBO crashes to the floor in bafflement **and** silence. His body and the poet's body align and twitch twice as the thunder roars.)

BERTRAND RUSSELL:
And then--the you is withdrawn... [CP]

(**ELIOT & COLOMBO EACH EXTEND AN ARM UPWARD. THE EKG MONITOR WHINES & FLATLINES. ELIOT'S ARM FALLS TO THE LEFT—COLOMBO'S ARM TO THE RIGHT.**)

SILENCE & DARKNESS...

VIVIENNE HAIGH-WOOD (VO FROM DARKNESS):
Shantihhhhhhhhhhhhhhhhhhhhhhhhhhhhhhhhhhhhhhhhhhhhh... [434]

AFTER A BEAT, IMMEDIATE ORCHESTRAL INTERLUDE:

"Sitting On Top of the World" A live band **marches down the AISLES OF THE LIVE THEATER** to the orchestral pit.

LIGHTS UP on the principals. They are dressed in black with white masks. ACTRESS B lounges on top of Eliot's Casket. She begins singing as the casket is rolled to **FRONT STAGE**.

ACTRESS B (SINGING):
I'm sitting on top of the world
Just rolling along just rolling along
I'm quitting the blues of the world
Just singing a song, just singing a song.

ACTORS A, C, & D (SINGING):
Glory Hallelujah, we just phoned the Parson
Hey, *Par* get ready to call.

ACTOR A (SINGING):
Just like Humpty Dumpty, I'm going to fall.

ACTRESS B (SINGING):
I'm sitting on top of the world
Just rolling along, just rolling along.

ACTORS A, B, C, & D (SINGING):
We're sitting on top of the world
Just rolling along, just rolling along
We're quitting the blues of the world
Just singing a song, just singing a song.

2nd **ORCHESTRAL INTERLUDE:**
"Toot, Toot, Tootsie, Goodbye" The band plays the jocular melody. The principals attach an overhead, descending hook to the back end of the casket.

Casket is raised perpendicularly upon the stage.
Its lid now beckons as a sealed door to a tomb.

ACTOR A (SINGING):
Yesterday I heard a lot of sighs,
Goodbye, oh me oh my...
We've come here from the village up ahead
To certify the bastard's really dead...

ACTORS B, C & D (SINGING):
Toot, Toot, Tootsie Goodbye / Toot, Toot, Tootsie don't cry /
Give me, give me, give me and then Baby, do it again...

(ACTOR A pries at the lid of the casket with the
point of his umbrella.)

ACTORS B, C, & D (SINGING):
And if he fails to find the poet's heart /
We can always drive the stake into his art /
Toot, Toot, Tootsie Goodbye.

81

(ACTOR A succeeds in prying the coffin ajar.
The lid swings open. The coffin is empty.)

ACTORS A, B, C & D (SINGING):
Toot, Toot, Tootsie - Oh My!

FINALE
Strobe-Flashing Crosses rise from Center Stage.
Thunder, fireworks & rain fill the rear scrim.
Band reprises principal melody of "APRIL SHOWERS".
ACTOR A opens and releases his Umbrella.
SPOT follows OPEN UMBRELLA slowly lifting.
It wafts through the cascading showers to
a cloudless empyrean ascending ...

ACTORS A, B, C & D (SINGING):
Toot, Toot, Tootsie - GOODBYE!

DARKNESS & CURTAIN

END

ACKNOWLEGEMENT

THE COMPLETE POEMS AND PLAYS
1909-1950
OF
THOMAS STEARNS ELIOT

*KEY TO THE 200 + LINES INCORPORATED IN THE PLAY:

PROFROCK (1917):

THE LOVE SONG OF J. ALFRED PRUFROCK (LS)
PRELUDES (P)
RHAPSODY ON A WINDY NIGHT (R)
MR. APOLLINAX (A)

POEMS (1920):

GERONTION (G)
BURBANK WITH A BAEDEKER: BLEISTEIN
WITH A CIGAR. (B)
SWEENY ERECT (SWE)
WHISPERS OF IMMORTALITY (W)
SWEENY AMONG THE NIGHTINGALES (SWN)

THE WASTE LAND (1922) LINES 1 - 434:

I.   THE BURIAL OF THE DEAD
II.   A GAME OF CHESS
III.   THE FIRE SERMON
IV   DEATH BY WATER
V   WHAT THE THUNDER SAID

THE WASTE LAND PREFACE (WLP)
THE WASTE LAND NOTES (N)
THE WASTE LAND EDIT: (WLE)
THE WASTE LAND EPIGRAPH (WLEP)

THE HOLLOW MEN (1925) (RM)

ASH WEDNESDAY (1930) (AW)

ARIEL POEMS:

MARINA **(M)**

UNFINISHED POEMS:

SWEENY AGONISTES (SWA) CORIOLAN (C)

MINOR POEMS:

FIVE-FINGER EXERCISES (FFE) LINES FOR AN OLD
MAN (LOM)

FOUR QUARTETS:

BURNT NORTON (BN)
EAST COKER (EC)
THE DRY SALVAGES (DS)
LITTLE GIDDING (LG)

MURDER IN THE CATHEDRAL (MC)
THE FAMILY REUNION (FR)
THE COCKTAIL PARTY (CP)

* *The Jolly Tinker (JJ)* and *Captain Colombo* verses were not included in any collections authorized by the poet. They survived *in* Ezra Pound's papers collected at the Beinecke Rare Book and Manuscript Library, Yale. *The Love Song of Saint Sebastian* (Sebastian) is *pre-Prufrock* and not in the standard collection.

APPENDIX

SETS

ELIOT'S OFFICE
FABER & FABER

ELIOT'S CHILDHOOD HOME
MYCENAE ON THE MISSOURI

TOM, VIV, & BERTIE

MAURICE HAIGH-WOOD

JEAN VERDENAL
(MAYHAPS)

POPE INNOCENT X
(FRANCIS BACON AFTER VELAZQUEZ)

1949 PORTRAIT OF ELIOT
PATRICK HERON

NOVEMBER 1963

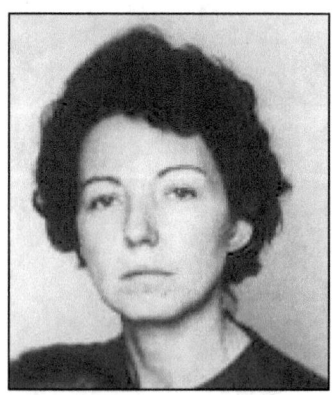

THREE WIDOWS
JACKIE, MARINA, MARIE

THE MAN FROM LLOYDS

A PRESLEY PASSION

ENACTMENT

A Presley Passion was first produced by Barbara Marcum as
A Passion for Elvis Aron Presley
for Cinda Jackson's Lost Studio in May and June of 2006.

Colonel Tom Parker: Dave Parke
Elvis: Ben Baker
Elvis: Seamus Frawley
Vernon Presley: Lance Fogan
Priscilla Presley: Susana Montal
Johann Sebastian Bach: Robin Jackson
Lighting : Scott Chamberlin
Lighting: Mario Gallegos
Director: M.C. Gardner

ELVIS: 95

A PRESLEY PASSION

ENACTMENT

DRAMATIS PERSONAE

GLOSS

NOTE ON THE MULTIPLE ROLES

NOTE ON THE WARDROBE

NOTE ON THE COLONEL

ENTR'ACTE

DRAMATIS PERSONAE:
FIVE ACTORS PLAYING MULTIPLE ROLES:

1. COLONEL TOM PARKER / YAHWEH
2. DOCTOR TERRENCE STEIN / ELVIS ARON PRESLEY
3. NURSE JANET MCCARREN / PRISCILLA PRESLEY / ANNE BOYLEN / ANNA
4. DOCTOR ENGEL / VERNON PRESLEY / ABRAHAM / MOSES / HENRY VIII
5. DOCTOR LEONARD KOPEL / J.S. BACH / CARDINAL THOMAS WOLSEY

GLOSS

Greil Marcus once wrote: "The controlling reason why it is so hard to think about Elvis is that his achievement--was seemingly so out of proportion to his means. Continents of meaning shifted according to certain gestures made on a television show, according to a few vocal hesitations on a handful of 45s. No one knows how to think of such a thing."

The approach to the Elvis mythos is told almost exclusively from point of view of his manager, Colonel Tom Parker. It should be noted that Parker's committal to *Asylum Saint Sophia* is fiction and that his possible involvement in a homicide a researched conjecture of biographer Alanna Nash. Parker's dismissal from the U.S. Army for Psychopathology is, however, a matter of medical record. Most what follows takes place upon the floorboards of the Colonel's dementia. Therein, he imagines that his health care providers are the Presley clan--Elvis, Vernon and Priscilla. A therapy of readings from the Bible to Dostoevsky and a recorded performance of Bach's Mass in B-Minor so inspires the Colonel that he feels exalted like a God though remaining tethered, as are we all, to a finitude fast concluding in the retreat of every heart beat

The date is January 8, 1997. Parker will be dead within two weeks. For the present, however, he is about to entertain an unexpected, albeit celebrated guest...

NOTE ON THE MULTIPLE ROLES:

With the exception of the hospital personnel, in Act I, the "multiple" characters are all fragments of the Colonel's shattered psyche. In Act II, the Colonel will find use even for the doctors within his mental derangement.

The major psychic fragments are memories of the Presley clan: Elvis, Priscilla and Vernon. The Colonel was autocratic and lorded over the Presleys like a stern, demanding father. Psychically they are also repressed aspects of the Colonel's own childhood. To a paranoid personality these fragments appear often as plotters that must be manipulated and controlled. They are also agents of truth that the Colonel must hold at bay.

100

NOTE ON THE WARDROBE:

Colonel parker is dressed in white and wears a straw hat(See appendix). The doctors and nurse McCarren are dressed in black shirts and pants with a long white medical over shirt. The medical shirt comes off when they are transformed by the Colonel's imagination into the other characters of the play. Bach wears the traditional long powdered tresses of the 18th century

NOTE ON THE COLONEL:

It should be further noted that the Colonel's attack on Julia Child is purely a conceit of the play.

ELVIS

A PRESLEY PASSION

M.C. GARDNER

JACK LANGGUTH

whose

Jesus Christs

is

Providential

ENTR'ACTE
PROJECTION ON SCREEN

I was flyin' back from Lubbock /
I saw Jesus on the plane /
Or maybe it was Elvis --
You know they kinda look the same.

Don Henley

ACT I

SCENE 1:

LIGHT CUE: LIGHTS UP.

Two crosses are conjoined making a letter H. Gruenwald's *Ascension* hangs beneath the crossbeam of the crosses. Three doctors flank a patient secured in straitjacket. The patient sits listlessly in his wheelchair.

DOCTOR KOPEL:
Any change?

DOCTOR ENGEL:
Catatonia is acute. Occasional spikes in brainwave activity have been noted. He remains, however, sequestered in silence.

DOCTOR KOPEL:
Doctor Engel, will you brief Doctor Stein?

DOCTOR STEIN:
Actually, Lennie, I've followed the Colonel's history for--

DOCTOR KOPEL:
Dr. Stein! Not every Leonard is a Lennie and despite your Oxford pedigree there are details of *that* history with which you are unfamiliar. Emil, please continue.

DOCTOR ENGEL:
Herr Parker was in consultation with Julia Child over his new book: *The Virginia Rib: A Gentleman's Art of the Barbeque.* Frau Child was to provide the Introduction. Everything was going so nicely, she simply noted that the contracts were being drawn on the birthday of Elvis Presley. Something snapped! He attacked and beat Julia with...

DOCTOR ENGEL (BECOMING EMOTIONALLY OVER WROUGHT): --with ah-hem, a marinated leg of lamb! (WEEPING AT THE THOUGHT) She was 84 years old. Mother Engel so loved that woman...

DOCTOR KOPEL:
It's alright, Emil--buck up, Doctor. Through efforts such as your own she returned to her soups and saintly soufflés--

DOCTOR ENGEL:
Danke, Herr Doctor.

DOCTOR KOPEL:
Today is the anniversary of that unfortunate episode.

DOCTOR ENGEL:
The Presley estate handled the settlement with Frau Child. It was everyone's desire to keep the matter strictly confidential.

DOCTOR KOPEL:
To this day the press believes Parker to be resting in the quiet seclusion of his Spanish Oakes estate and no one in this hospital shall give them reason to suspect otherwise. *Terry*, would you ask the nurse of primary care to join us?

DOCTOR STEIN:
Nurse McCarren...

NURSE MCCARREN:
Yes, Doctor?

DOCTOR KOPEL:
I see in your notes that, aside from his interest in *Barbeque,* that the Colonel was a history buff and an avid bibliophile.

NURSE MCCARREN:
I read to him daily from *The Brothers Karamazov* and the *Weekly World News.*

DOCTOR KOPEL:

Let's dispense with the tabloids and please keep the Russian to a minimum--I'd like to address a more traditionally spiritual side...

NURSE MCCARREN:

Aloysha is deeply--

DOCTOR KOPEL:

A minimum! Say we start with Luke 24. After that mix it up any way you like. Gruenwald's painting is allusive...

PROJECT
GRUENWALD'S RESURRECTION:
APPENDIX 1

DOCTOR KOPEL:

The risen Christ ascends from the darkness of a stone sarcophagus. Think of our patient as so constrained. He must push away a stone to find his way home. St. Luke's as good a guide as any. Don't be afraid to jazz it up a bit. I want the readings to stimulate what remains of the patient's consciousness. I would like to, as well, begin a regimen of music therapy for Mr. Parker.

DOCTOR STEIN:

Music therapy? Sunday school readings? For God's sake, Kopel, this is the man that crucified the career of Elvis Presley! *Parker's* not even his real name.

DOCTOR KOPEL:

Be that as it may, Doctor, he is not a monster. He is 87 years old and entitled to the best care we can provide. Janet, how many months have you monitored Mr. Parker?

NURSE MCCARREN:

I began my residency on the day of the Colonel's arrival. I feel an intimacy that I can't quite explain. I believe there's more to the Colonel than we have yet to fully explore.

DOCTOR KOPEL:
The exploration begins today. Doctor Engel will prescribe an appetite enhancement--I'd like to wean him from the *I.V.* Please let me know of any metabolic aberrations.

NURSE MCCARREN:
Yes, Doctor.

DARKNESS

TITLE CARD PROJECTED ON SCREEN:

LUKE 24

NURSE MCCARREN (VO):
"Now on the first day of the week... they came to the tomb of Jesus to sweeten his broken flesh *with spices. But they found* **the stone rolled away and the tomb empty..."**

LIGHT CUE: SLOW LIGHTS UP

SCENE 2:

> **A hunched figure has appeared in PARKER'S HOSPITAL ROOM. As the COLONEL raises his head, the golem-like creature rises to its full stature. DOCTOR STEIN is transformed into the *King of Rock and Roll*, ELVIS ARON PRESLEY, his hospital smock replaced by the black leather ensemble of the '68 special. Elvis cocks his head as if trying to coax a sound from the silence.**

ELVIS:
Momma, momma, is that you, momma? It's so cold. I'm sorry, momma, I took his breath at his death, but I never meant to kill him.

> (COLONEL PARKER rises from his wheelchair.
> His strait-jacket falling freely to the floor.)

COLONEL TOM PARKER:
Son, you can't take what the dead don't have.

> (He puts on one of his signature white straw hats and continues talking as he walks to his former charge.)

COLONEL TOM PARKER:
I'm neither your mammy nor your pappy but I can tell you this-- your little brother was born without a heartbeat. He was stone cold when they laid him down upon your mother's teat. Why...

> (The COLONEL whispers a salacious comment to ELVIS. ELVIS becomes enraged and begins to strangle his former manager. The COLONEL breaks free.)

COLONEL TOM PARKER:
You damn fool, (COUGHING) it's me--it's the Colonel!

ELVIS:
... My poor mother...

COLONEL TOM PARKER:
I'm sorry. (COUGHING AND THEN BOTH HANDS OVER HEART) I apologize. That crack was in bad taste but I've never known any other. Son, we've had our differences (COUGHING) but for a couple of hours you'd well served to set them aside. I hear it whispered about that I'm certifiably insane and then your dead ass appears in my hospital suite and I gets to thinking: With you moldering in the grave and me locked in a *loony bin* we're well-poised to make a killing! Hell, the world won't know what the fuck's hit 'em. I've got one more gig under my hat, then you'll be free--I can promise you that. We're going to Vegas to shoot a play-- a *Passion Play*, a requiem for *your* well-documented sins. After that you can go wherever you please. I'll ask around about your mammy--it looks to me like nothing would make Gladys more proud than to see you back on top. Elvis, it's time to think about a comeback--the only thing that stands between you, your momma, and *eternal glory* is a signature.

(He hands ELVIS a pen & clipboard from the wheelchair. ELVIS takes the pen and after a beat begins to sign. At STAGE LEFT J.S. BACH mounts a wood podium. He holds a conductor's baton and his head is bowed.)

COLONEL TOM PARKER CONT'D:
Now don't bother with the fine print, just dot the *eyes* and cross the *titties*. That's it, E--good job, good job. (HE TAKES, FOLDS AND KISSES THE DOCUMENT.) Beautiful--(THE COLONEL BEGINS TO LAUGH TO HIMSELF.)

COLONEL TOM PARKER (CONT'D):
I say son, I say screw the '68 Special.
This ain't no Rock 'n Roll, boy and that *Krout* over there with the dread locks ain't no Rastafarian. We're going 1st class and we ain't ever turning back. This is going to be huge; this is going to be the goddamn *2nd Coming*!

> **SOUND CUE: BACH BEGINS KYRIE ELEISON**
> **NIGHT CUE: DARKNESS AFTER 10 SEC**
>
> **PROJECT**
> **ELVIS, GLADYS AND VERNON NATIVITY**
> **APPENDIX 2**
>
> **LIGHT CUE: LIGHTS UP AT CONCLUSION**

SCENE 3:

COLONEL TOM PARKER:
Elvis, down on the volume--we don't want J.S. to blow the Hilton's speakers.

ELVIS:
The Hilton people know you, Colonel. It's always been *your* show.

COLONEL TOM PARKER:
Shit, they'll bill me one way or t'other.

ELVIS:
Don't be scared, Colonel...

COLONEL TOM PARKER:
Scared? Why son, that's just plain ignorant. Those cocksuckers are afraid of me!

ELVIS:
They can't touch you, Colonel——*they're* the ones beholding.

COLONEL TOM PARKER:
That's God's truth, son--lips to ears, let's pray he hears. Alright, E, after the red light flashes...

ELVIS:
I know, Colonel——last chance, last dance. I'm coming out... My name is Elvis Aron Presley. Sometimes, just E or El, depending on the affection in which I'm held. This feels like my first appearance at a dairy show in Tupelo, Mississippi. I was ten years old and didn't even own a guitar. Later they called me King but that's next to nothing--family is the only thing that matters. I'm descended from Abraham Lincoln and a Cherokee princess. I'm father to Lisa Marie and twin (PAUSE) twin to Jesse Garon Presley. My brother died upon the cross of his deliverance in a Mississippi manger, January 8, 1935. I was born half an hour later. The second "A" in my middle name was dropped in tribute to the twin who was cut lifeless from my side. Jesse *Garon* was buried in a shoebox; his body laid in an unmarked grave. I died on August 16, 1977--my heart had failed but it had long since been broken. They put back the missing "A" on my grave stone...

PROJECT
ELVIS GRAVESTONE
APPENDIX 3

ELVIS(CONT'D):
as if at my journey's end I could again begin. This January 8th the Colonel's given me leave to sort out the details of my redemption the only way I know:

SOUND CUE: *HUSH LITTLE BABY*

ELVIS (SINGING):
So hush little baby don't you cry You know your daddy's bound to die

ELVIS (SPEAKING):
There aren't any clocks in this theatre. The air and the lights have been adjusted like the home I once called Graceland.

MUSIC CUE: *DIXIE*

ELVIS(SINGING):
Oh I wish I was in the land of cotton. Old times there are not forgotten. Look away. Look away. Look away Dixie land.

ELVIS:
The book I was reading when I passed was called *The Search for the Face of Jesus.* But it is here that I've come looking for a face lost long ago in time--today *our Father who art in Hilton* is Colonel Tom Parker (HE STANDS). He's written a play. He calls it a *Passion Play*--for me and my family. Priscilla spent last night at the Hilton (NURSE MCCARREN STANDS SANS WHITE MEDICAL OVER SHIRT).She believes this is a dream——she used to think that when we were first married but she's a good sport and has agreed to **play along.** Our Musical Director is Mr. J. Sebastian Bach...

> (DOCTOR KOPEL REMOVES HIS WHITE MEDICAL OVERCOAT AND DONS HIS WHITE POWDERED WIG. HE STANDS)

ELVIS(CONT'D):
and our spiritual needs are tended by Cardinal Thomas Wolsey, whose over yonder in the confessional. My daddy plays the father figures of the drama (DOCTOR ENGEL STANDS WITHOUT WHITE MEDICAL OVER SHIRT). Vernon's been a comfort since his own passing in '79--we hope to, one day, find our mother Gladys. Mayhaps she and little Jesse will join us here today and I'll be free at last, free at last, great God almighty I'll be home free at last.

MUSIC CUE: *DIXIE* CONCLUDED

ELVIS(SINGING):
But all my trials, Lord, will soon be over. {Next line spoken over
Flute solo}: That's Peter Riley on the flute, good job Pete.(ELVIS
SINGING):Look away. Look away. Look away. To Dixieland.")

(BACH MOUNTS BOX PODIUM)

ELVIS:
On the wings of that prayer, I send my love to heaven in a song...

MUSIC CUE ON DOWNBEAT:
SANCTUS

LIGHT CUE: AFTER 30 SECONDS:
DARKNESS.

MUSIC CONTINUES IN DARKNESS.

A TITLE CARD IS PROJECTED:

ISENHEIM STATIONS:
Colmar, France

NATIVITY
DEATH – ASCENSION

PROJECT
IN TURN
THREE PANELS OF GRUNEWALD'S ALTAR PIECE
APPENDIX 4,5,6

THE FINAL PANEL ILLUMINATES TO A
BLINDING BRILLIANT WHITE...

SCENE 4:

TITLE CARD PROJECTED ON SCREEN:
GENESIS 1

NURSE MCCARREN (VO):
"In the beginning Elohim created the heavens and the earth. And the earth was without form and void; and darkness was upon the face of the deep. And Elohim said let there be light and there was light!"

LIGHT CUE: LIGHTS UP

COLONEL TOM PARKER:
Excellent! (CALLING OUT TO HER) Priscilla, Priscilla, have you got the new pages?

> (NURSE MCCARREN takes off her white medical over-shirt and is transformed into PRISCILLA PRESLEY.)

PRISCILLA:
I'm waiting on *you*, Colonel.

COLONEL TOM PARKER:
Here you are, Princess. There's also a release form that requires your signature. It's the usual estate bullshit--not much to it.

> (He hands her the paperwork. She signs it.
> He takes, folds and puts it in his pocket.)

COLONEL TOM PARKER (CONT'D)
Lovely, Elvis and I are so glad to have you aboard.

PRISCILLA:
Someone said you were sick--but I don't believe it.

COLONEL TOM PARKER:
I'm as hungry as a grizzly--but sick?

(LAUGHING AND COUGHING)

COLONEL TOM PARKER(CONT'D)
Well, dear (COUGHING) that's a bee best kept under your bonnet.

PRISCILLA:
The Marquee read: *"Dead Elvis, Live!"* Then I woke up and wandered down a hallway to a stage I've never seen--and then I saw him! Elvis lives as if the Colonel rolled away a stone so he'd not be left alone. It's a long way back to Graceland and deeper South to Tupelo. I see him often as a mist dissolving in a mirror.

PRISCILLA (SINGING ACAPELLA):
You know I can be found, sitting all alone if you can't come around. At least please telephone ...

PRISCILLA:
Lisa Marie says that daddy's on the highway trying to hitch a ride but the off-ramp to *Forever* never brings us to his side...

COLONEL TOM PARKER:
That's touching, dear, but please, keep to the material at hand-- thank you, honey.

PRISCILLA:
Elvis, sometimes I think the Colonel knows what I'm going to say before I say it.

ELVIS:
It's a trick he learned on the *circuit*.

PRISCILLA:
The carnival?

ELVIS:
His Uncle's *Dog and Pony Show*--a *front* for bear-baiting *and* bingo. My daddy worked there one summer. He fed the bears and ran the numbers.

116

PRISCILLA:
Someone once called him the "Snowman."

ELVIS:
That's right, Cilla--no one could "snow" you like the Colonel. During the day the Colonel ran a cemetery for the "perpetual care of beloved dead pets." I guess I'm numbered among 'em.

PRISCILLA:
Elvis, the Colonel always said that you would never die--from then to now--I've never wondered why.

> (ELVIS takes her hand and kisses
> the back of her fingers.)

LIGHT CUE: LIGHTS DOWN

> (VERNON PRESLEY, the former DOCTOR
> ENGEL, is called upon to play the father figures
> of the COLONEL'S "play."

SCENE 5:

**PROJECT TITLE CARD:
GENESIS 22**

NURSE MCCARREN (VO):
"Now after these things, it came about that Elohim did tempt Abraham and said unto him:

LIGHT CUE: LIGHTS UP

COLONEL TOM PARKER (VO):
Abraham!

VERNON (WAKING FROM DOWN STAGE)
Aghhhh. Leave me alone.

COLONEL TOM PARKER (V0)
Vernon, it's the Colonel--hear my word and pick up the damn script!

VERNON:
Colonel, you old varmint--let me sleep.

COLONEL TOM PARKER (VO):
Would that I might, but thou hast slept through most of thy life.

> (The COLONEL joins "ABRAHAM" on the
> stage of the HILTON.)

COLONEL TOM PARKER:
Don't get up--thou wilt be better served if I continue as a dream--
never look directly at me.

> (VERNON sits up. He wipes the
> darkness from his eyes.)

VERNON:
What is it, Colonel?

COLONEL TOM PARKER:
On Friday next, thou shalt make thy way in darkness to the
Mountains of Moriah. When the fingers of the dawn tweak the
nipples of the night thou shalt rise and make of thy first born an
offering to thy Colonel. Abraham -- dost thou understand?

VERNON:
Jesse, has long since been lost to me.

COLONEL TOM PARKER:
Please, Vern--you're confusing memory with myth--today thou art
Father Abraham and I am the Lord thy God. But truth to tell,
Vern--I'm having a god-awful week. Priscilla's lawyers cut my
percentage off at the knees; the Pritikin people tell me that my
cholesterol is up; and then Princeton wires that the Universe is
winding down. The one thing I thought I could count on! Elvis,
my pills!

(Enter ELVIS dropping pills on the stage...)

ELVIS (OFFERING PILLS FROM A BOWL):
Right here, Colonel.

COLONEL TOM PARKER:
Idiot! My nerves are going to pieces and *my* doctors don't pass out Seconal like Halloween candy.

> (The COLONEL grabs a handful of the pill & puts them in his mouth.)

COLONEL TOM PARKER (MUMBLING AND GAGING):
Ge-zeus H. Fuhking Chrisss ! Waaaaaaater!

> (ELVIS hands him a cup of water. The Colonel gags and spews water and pills on the stage or spittoon.)

COLONEL TOM PARKER:
91,000 pills in the Vegas years alone. (COUGHING AND TAKING A DEEP BREATH) When you finally *kicked* you'd taken enough *Ludes* to down a pachyderm. A creature you had come to somewhat resemble.(PAUSE AND BREATH) Abe old boy, is it any wonder that I need a change of pace or palette. For some time now thy lambs have proved a trifle gamey and it's clear thy fatted calves have lost their zing! I've always said that the only thing that stands between me and the future is another meal. Abraham, dost thou *now* understand what I ask of thee?

VERNON:
Colonel--I am thy servant.

COLONEL TOM PARKER:
Vernon, thou not only sired Elvis but as Abraham thou art the father of a people. The people of my book -- my cook book! Thou art to roll the boy in herbs and butterfat, lay him gently upon the Altar Stone and then slit the lad from nave to neck and toss his entrails steaming to the desert sand!

119

VERNON:
Colonel, would thou have a father crucify a son?

COLONEL TOM PARKER:
Silence! Crucifixion should only be attempted by a redoubtable chef. It is Italian and best served with pesto and antipasti. (WITH GROWING VIOLENCE) Who are thee, little man, to question the dictates of thy Colonel? Where wast thou when I set the cornerstones of the earth, dropped a plumb line from the stars and took Elvis for 50%? Speak! If thou knowest, or I swear on the souls of thy sleeping ancestors that thou wilt be the next steak stretched across the stone!

VERNON:
My Lord overwhelms me.

COLONEL TOM PARKER:
Yes, of course I do. Now as to the disposition of the meat: carve from the hindquarters a hunk of the consecrated flesh; spit on a turning spike and roast until brown; taking care, of course, not to burn the buns.

VERNON:
My tongue thickens in my mouth.

COLONEL TOM PARKER:
Hmmm, mine too. Season the meat with garlic and roasted chestnuts. Braise the boy with chicken broth and brandy. Hast thou got that? Elvis will provide a copy of the recipe.

VERNON:
I am bereft of speech.

COLONEL TOM PARKER:
Wonderful! I'm so glad we've had this chat. Loanne and I will see you on the morning of the Sabbath, next. Shall we say *sevenish*?

VERNON:
Yes, my Lord.

COLONEL TOM PARKER:
Very well, then. Please be on time and be sure that Jesse--I'm sorry--be sure that *Isaac* is dressed and properly garnished.

(The COLONEL and VERNON exit.
Enter ELVIS and PRISCILLA.)

ELVIS:
Talking about Jesse will mess with my daddy's head.

PRISCILLA:
The Colonel's a sad little man. He's too unhappy to be kind -- to either your kin or to mine.

(VERNON stands alone, UPSTAGE. He feels the chill of a distant memory. ELVIS appears in the shadows behind him. He subsumes the identity of JESSE/ISAAC. VERNON and ELVIS face forward.)

ELVIS:
Father?

VERNON:
Yes? (LISTENING) Jesse, is that you?

ELVIS:
Here is the kindling for the fire. I have sharpened the knife as thou requested. Look, I cut my finger. Where is the offering we are to burn?

VERNON:
God will provide the lamb, my son.

**LIGHT CUE: DARKNESS
FOR 1ST VERSE**

**PROJECT
BLACK LEATHER ELVIS
APPENDIX 7**

SOUND CUE: *MYSTERY TRAIN*

ELVIS (VO):
Train I Ride / 16 coaches long / Train I ride /16 coaches long. / "Well that long black train took my baby and gone.

LIGHTS UP: ELVIS CONTINUES (ON STAGE), SEATED WITH GUITAR:

ELVIS (SINGING):
Train train, comin' round the bend. Train Train, comin' round the bend / Well it took my baby but it never well again.
    (ELVIS (SPOKEN BEHIND INSTRUMENTAL BRIDGE):

ELVIS:
Say hello to Bill Black on electric bass. He and Scotty were with me at the beginning. He died of a brain tumor in '65--I love *ya*, Bill. It's is good to have Mr. Black at my back. My momma read me from the Bible when I was just a little baby. I don't remember chapter and verse--but just being with my momma was more important than anything I ever read:

MUSIC CUE: *THAT'S ALL RIGHT MOMMA*

ELVIS (SINGING):
Well that's all right, momma / that's all right for you. That's all right momma, just anyway you do.
Well that's all right, that's all right, that's all right now momma anyway you do...

ELVIS (CONT'D):
Sometimes I feel she's near--and that I'll find her and little Jesse just beyond the crossroads at the next whistle-stop along the way. I can her voice telling me to be a good boy where ever my fortunes might lead...

MUSIC & PHOTO CUE: THAT'S ALRIGHT MOMMA

ELVIS (SINGING):
*Mama she done told me / Papa done told me too / Son that gal your foolin'
with she ain't no good for you.*
*But that's all right, that's all right / that's all right my momma any way you
do...*

COLONEL TOM PARKER:
Son, the lighting is better for Priscilla, Down Stage. We lost her a
couple of times in the shadows.

ELVIS:
Lost her, Colonel?

COLONEL TOM PARKER:
She's fine, son. I think for the interiors we'll go with a Number
Two filter——yes, that's better. Quiet, everyone.

**(LISTENING
SOUND CUE: ALARM)**

COLONEL TOM PARKER:
Clear the stage--someone is coming down the hall.

(The COLONEL returns to his wheelchair and
catatonia.)

SCENE 6:

**NURSE MCCARREN enters in breathless
excitement...**

NURSE MCCARREN:
Colonel, I couldn't wait to see you. It says here that astronomers
have spotted a giant statue of Elvis on Jupiter's 2nd largest moon! A
souvenir and gift shop are soon to follow ...

DOCTOR KOPEL:
Ohhhhhh, Janet? Anything?

(NURSE MCCARREN hides the tabloid.)

NURSE MCCARREN:
I've been alternating the Presley Canon with the Mass. His blood pressure rises when I read the King James. I "jazz" it up whenever I can...

DOCTOR KOPEL:
It's a beginning. I have some coffee brewing in the office and the *Well Tempered Clavier* is on *KCLASSICS*. The Gould recording will long remain the gold-standard. Feel free to drop by.

NURSE MCCARREN:
Thank you, Doctor.

DOCTOR KOPEL:
And Janet?

NURSE MCCARREN:
Yes, Doctor.

DOCTOR KOPEL:
It might be best to leave Elvis on whatever planet or in which ever Deli that the tabloids have sighted him.

NURSE MCCARREN:
The King James, Doctor?

DOCTOR KOPEL:
Thank you, Janet...

LIGHT CUE:
LIGHTS DOWN

PROJECTION ON SCREEN:
EXODUS 3

NURSE McCARREN (VO):
"And Moses became a shepherd of the flock of Jethro and he drove a flock to the mountain of Yahweh where he rested until morning."

LIGHT CUE: LIGHTS UP
SOUND CUE: PHONE RINGS
FIVE TIMES

(COLONEL PARKER searches for the missing phone.)

COLONEL TOM PARKER:
Jesus, Mary and Joesph DiMaggio, where's the damn phone? Elvis? Elvis? You there, boy? (LISTENING) For *Chrissakes,* E -- you're hopeless! Get me that broad from *A T and Tease!* Hello, operator? That's right, person to person--I don't need no dish--I've got a bush wired and burning on Sinai--thanks, doll. Ring me when you've got the Hebrew...

(He hangs up the phone down. He twists his head to relieve a tension cramp in his neck.)

COLONEL TOM PARKER:
Moses ... *Moses supposes*--that there's a gator in the grass or a bull in the rushes, but I assure thee, son--except for Elvis and thy sheep, this morning thou art quite alone. Coffee? Croissant?

VERNON:
Colonel-- Abraham or Moses?--make up your mind.

COLONEL TOM PARKER:
Each of us plays many roles in the fiction of time. The creator was Yahweh in Judah, and as Elohim, perhaps a multitude of gods in Israel. Be he one or many he is a God of many guises. Thy Colonel is only a latterly addition to a long, long list. That is the *First Lesson,* of two, that I shall grant thee this day. Listen, Vern, and learn.

(The COLONEL hands him a pair of sunglasses.)

COLONEL TOM PARKER:
Here, these will shield thee from my splendor. Moses, I have heard thy people's cry and I arrive with plagues, poetry, and the best damn script since Faulkner penned *Land of the Pharaohs* for those Jew-boys over at Warners. Would you like to take a peek? Elvis baby!

ELVIS:
Right here, Colonel.

VERNON:
Colonel, don't take that tone with my boys——the quick or the dddddddddddddead!

COLONEL TOM PARKER:
Vernon, pleeeeeeease--*you* are not the *quick* and *both* your boys are dead. I speak to each of you no better or worse than your *desserts* deserve! I don't suppose you've got any Jack Daniels in that knapsack. No? Now that would be a miracle! You see, Moe in the general scheme of things, *Man* has never rated higher than the Jackal, let alone the Daniels. It's all been bad luck--not far from *In the beginning.*

VERNON:
Luuuuuuuuuuck?

COLONEL TOM PARKER:
Bad luck--like your stutter, Moe, is the Darwinian insult of bad blood and botched chemistry. I wanted the earth simply for the rocks. Rocks are quiet, well-behaved, unassuming, and sometimes sparkle, quite charmingly in the dark. I poisoned the planet with ammonia and carbon dioxide so that nothing would muck up "me" rocks and the next thing you know...

VERNON:
Every llllllllliving thing?

COLONEL TOM PARKER:
I turn my back for an eon and the world's a mess with lichen and moss. You ever try to clean lichen off a rock? Well, son it's not pretty.

VERNON:
And Adam?

COLONEL TOM PARKER:
The biggest train wreck of creation! Witness your son, an erstwhile *King*. It's not as if the lad went without instruction. I taught the boy everything he knew down to the last shake of his squirrelly behind.

VERNON:
I learned him at home. Elvis was good boy and I applied a birch branch to his butt no more than two or three times a year. Gladys taught him his prayers.

COLONEL TOM PARKER:
"Men's prayers are a disease of the will...their creeds, a disease of the intellect." That's Emerson, son--he used to drink my grand daddy under the table *back in the day*. Ralph Waldo was hard man to shut down once you got him *Reverend Up*. Gramps used to say that prayer was a *grift* and every priest was a *shill*. The first will plead for Heaven and the second, give you Hell! Ask any altar boy buggered in a sacristy or buggered in a cell, buggery so common that it's hardly worth the *tell*. That kinda of talk got the two of them thrown out of half the taverns in Concord. But *Ralphie-boy* had a point. To put a nickel in one pocket I must empty another. You have to empty a lot of pockets to buy a car lot of Caddies -- 14 Cadillacs in a single afternoon! Even for Elvis it was excessive.

VERNON:
I am nnnnnnnnothig without the boy...

> (The COLONEL pulls out a small
> notebook and checklist.)

COLONEL TOM PARKER:

Less, Vern — sssssssssssssssssssssubstantially less. In 1938 you were sent to the *hoosegow* for transforming a three dollar check into an eight dollar pay stub. Three years for five fucking dollars--small change and the pitiful poor!

VERNON:

They released me early—my boss was kinder than the *Feds* and asked for clemency. In '38 "five ffffffffffucking dollars" was bread and milk for a month. Something is lost in a man when his children go hungry. Something I couldn't put *back* on the table. I can't trump you, Colonel. What is thy bbbbbbbbbbidding?

COLONEL TOM PARKER:

Oh, just a sssssssssuggestion or two--and a signature on a simple contract. You and Elvis are to be handsomely compensated for an appearance as yourselves in a nearly completed *Passion Play*, for a run of unspecified duration. What could be simpler? You have over three thousand years to learn your lines.

VERNON:

I'll take that ccccccccccup of coffee.

COLONEL:

Now listen, Vern, and take note. Pharaoh's scriptwriters are the finest in the Levant. They will riddle thee witless before the first frog falls from the sky. But fear not. We'll beat De Mille at his own game. Thou art the *real* deal. Why, you're already in costume! Moses, we're talking limos the length of the Nile. A *New Jerusalem* paved in gold and lit up like Liberace in the desert night. We're talking dames, tits, and butts that bounce! Goddamn it, man, I made the heavens--I can make thee a Star!

> **MUSIC CUE**: *Viva Las Vegas.*
> The COLONEL accompanies ELVIS on *maracas*.

ELVIS:

Bright light city going set my soul/ going to set my soul on fire / I've got a whole lot of money that's ready to burn / so set those stakes up higher.

COLONEL TOM PARKER (SINGING):
There's a thousand pretty women awaiting out there / They're all living the devil may care / I'm just a devil with love to spare /

CHORUS:
Viva Las Vegas / Viva Las Vegas.

ELVIS (SINGING):
How I wish that there were more than 24 hours in a day / Even if there were 40 more I wouldn't let a moment slip away.

COLONEL TOM PARKER (SINGING):
Why there's Black Jack and Poker and the Roulette wheel / A fortune won and lost in every deal /

ELVIS (SINGING):
All you need's a strong heart and a nerve of steel /

CHORUS:
Viva Las Vegas, Viva Las Vegas, Viva, Viva Las Vegas.

COLONEL TOM PARKER:
Present your pappy with the paper work.

> (ELVIS gives Vernon the paperwork. VERNON signs and begins to read the fine print. The COLONEL snatches the document from him.)

COLONEL TOM PARKER:
Standard legalese, Moe--don't strain your eyes.

VERNON:
Colonel, if I removed these shades —— I might more clearly see thy ddddesign and handiwork...

COLONEL TOM PARKER:
Mayhaps thou might. But take care, Moses. Only those that know my face gleams with the silver of an infinite mirror need not fear the face they find within.

VERNON:
Perhaps if I ssssslowly opened my eyes?

COLONEL TOM PARKER:
Yes——but the truth is not without its dangers. Art thou certain that thy wish is commensurate with thy desire?

(All actors exit. Vernon enters the acting area.)

VERNON:
Yes, Colonel.

COLONEL TOM PARKER (VO):
Prepare thee thy witness...

BACH MOUNTS BOX AND DOWNBEAT
MUSIC CUE: Begin **"GRATIAS AGIMUS TIBI"**

From BACH'S MASS IN B-MINOR. VERNON
falls to his knees. He slowly raises his arms in
supplication to the music.
The music abruptly stops and:

LIGHT CUE: QUICK DARKNESS

VERNON (VO):
My God, I am alone in the dark!

(A flashlight held from below briefly
illuminates the COLONEL'S face.)

COLONEL TOM PARKER:
Yes Moses, and *that* is the second lesson...

FLASHLIGHT OFF--DARKNESS

END ACT 1

ENTR'ACTE
PROJECTION ON SCREEN

We made a hell of team. I thought we'd go on forever...

COLONEL TOM PARKER

ACT II

SCENE 1:

CAST ASSEMBLES:

DOCTOR ENGEL, NURSE MCCARREN, DOCTOR STEIN AND HERR BACH TAKE THEIR POSITIONS IN SEATS IN FRONT OF PODIUM AT STAGE RIGHT

LIGHT CUE: LIGHTS DOWN
LIGHT CUE: LIGHTS UP

KAPELLMEISTER BACH taps his baton on the podium. NURSE MCCARREN is on violin; DOCTOR ENGEL, on cello; and DOCTOR STEIN is the tenor soloist. They begin playing at the down beat.

SOUND CUE: *BENEDICTUS*
THE VIOLIN CARRIES THE MELODY; THE CELLO, THE ACCOMPANADO.

DOCTOR STEIN (SINGING):
Benedictus qui venit in nominee Domini.

LIGHT CUE: LIGHTS DOWN AFTER TENOR SOLO.

(VIOLIN AND CELLO CONTINUE IN DARKNESS TO CONCLUSION.)

DOCTORS KOPEL AND ENGEL EXIT.

LIGHT CUE: LIGHTS SLOWLY UP

(STEIN walks over to the COLONEL.)

DOCTOR STEIN:
Bunk! You hear me, Parker--Bach is bunk!

(STEIN pulls on Parker's left ear.)

DOCTOR STEIN:
Anybody home, Colonel? Any one ever home?

(DOCTOR STEIN lights a cigarette.)

DOCTOR STEIN (CONT'D):
"Colonel Tom Parker." The honor for which Governor Clement bestowed your title has been lost to the Tennessee historical record, buried, as it were, in the sands of time. You are not a Colonel, neither a Tom, nor a Parker. Who is Andreas Cornelius van Kuijk? Why the façade, Colonel? Is there anything at all behind those dead black eyes...

(STEIN blows a lungful of smoke in the COLONEL'S face. The COLONEL remains unresponsive.)

DOCTOR STEIN (CONT'D):
... or just the smoke and mirrors that are prelude to yet another con?

STEIN EXITS.

COLONEL TOM PARKER:
All right--who's the needle-dick that's been (COUGHING) been smoking a fuckin' cigarette? Elvis, match me!

(ELVIS lights the COLONEL'S cigar.)

ELVIS
Colonel, are you okay?

COLONEL TOM PARKER:
My throat's parched...(EXHALING A PUFF OF SMOKE)But I'm okay--I've got it under control.

133

ELVIS:
Beg your pardon, Colonel--I was dead at forty-two, under your control.

COLONEL TOM PARKER:
Say again, son?

ELVIS:
... forty-two.

ELVIS EXITS.

COLONEL TOM PARKER (SMOKING HIS CIGAR):
The King, alas, is dead. This thing that was the King now flies a little lower than the angels. Presidential pedigree, my ass! What the fuck *was* you but two-bit trailer trash from East Tupelo! (INHALING SMOKE FROM CIGAR.) Why your cousin Bobby was a suicide by rat poison; your uncle *Tic Tic* Tracy was a retard who believed he was a time bomb awaiting detonation. (RELEASING SMOKE IN A "KABOOM.") Tick, Tick, Tick... Kabooooooooooooooooooooooooooooooooom! And by God they were the pick of the litter! (LAUGHING LOUDLY THEN QUIET.) Little Jesse was buried in a blue suede shoe box--"small change and the pitiful poor" and you think your miserable talent kept you off the welfare dole! You goddamn pill-popping, pasty ass, prima-donna! Flash-in-the-pan Presley, that's what William Morris called you and that's just what *you'd a been* if I hadn't finessed your wet-dream vulgarity into something of class and distinction. I made you a gentleman, a true son of the South.

**PROJECT
ELVIS, GRACELAND & LIMO
APPENDIX 9**

COLONEL TOM PARKER (CONT'D):
That's a load, boy. Bullshit! High octane bullshit--a pile wide

(MORE)

COLONEL TOM PARKER (CONT'D):
stacked a mile high! Hell, half the kikes in the office thought you were as queer as the three dollar bills I passed in the 30s. At least being a goddamned cocksucker would have slowed you down some. But no, nothing could stop your bird dog pursuit of prom queen poontang.

PROJECT
PANTIES ALOFT
APPENDIX 10

COLONEL TOM PARKER (CONT'D):
You were diddling every teeny bopper with a ticket in one hand and her panties in *t'other*--you couldn't resist the wattage in their *twatage*. Either way the press would have eaten you alive if I hadn't kept them at bay. When you got your pathetic ass drafted that should have been the end of it. Fuck! I wouldn't let them forget you. Fuck! I made you a bigger star upon your return than you were before you left. Fuck, three pictures a year with Hal Wallis-- and not that *hoytie-toytie-crap* with Burton and O'Toole--my movies were guaranteed to turn a buck! Fuck! Without me you'd still be a hillbilly nigger trucking moonshine from the South of Carolina to the North of New Orleans. Fuck! Fuck you, you mother-fucking ingrate!

ELVIS:
Colonel--something about my mother?

COLONEL TOM PARKER:
Nothing, son. (CATCHING HIS BREATH) I was just thinking that... (PAUSE) that we ought to spot her, soon, somewhere here and about. Why don't you and Cilla *knockoff* for awhile. You're always stronger after a nap. You say your prayers--Gladys would like that. I'll have a look around and scope out what I can. Maybe I can rustle us up a little grub...

DARKNESS

135

SCENE 2:

TITLE CARD PROJECTION
I SAMUEL 18

NURSE MCCARREN (VO):
And it came to pass on the morrow, that the evil spirit of Elohim came upon Saul concerning the shepherd, David...

LIGHT CUE: LIGHTS SLOWLY UP
ON ELVIS PLAYING;
THE SHEPHERD DAVID

ELVIS:
Lord, do you hear me Lord?

COLONEL TOM PARKER:
What dost thou wish?

ELVIS:
Lord, the darkness and the quiet, deepens all around me. How am I to find my way home?

COLONEL TOM PARKER:
Thou must first become a hero; then, thyself, will ascend the throne of Israel--

ELVIS:
Is my momma there?

COLONEL TOM PARKER:
First, thou must slay the giant, Goliath.

ELVIS:
Will Jessie be with her?

COLONEL TOM PARKER:
King Saul will request of thee, a lyric--thy musical fame precedes thee.

ELVIS:
Will they forgive me, Colonel?

COLONEL TOM PARKER:
I have arranged for thee a nuptials. Thou wilt marry the King's daughter, Princess Priscilla--she's a bitch, but the ripest peach in the palace garden. Thou will woo her with your harp and a song. As to the King thou must first provide a dowry for the wench. King Saul will ask thee for three stones of prepuces.

ELVIS:
Pre-what?

COLONEL TOM PARKER:
Foreskins, son. We're not talking the partial castration of the "*spandone*", when only the gonads go--nor the "*castrato assolto*" where the infidel loses the whole cock *and caboodle*--no sir, here in Zion we incise only the extended circumference of the prepuce. Yes, three stones works out to be around one-hundred of the pesky portions--we, however will be generous suitors, and up the ante yet, one-hundred more. The King's appetite, albeit eccentric, is near boundless. Thou shall collect the bulk of the booty from uncircumcised infidels. I should think the Philistines are a good bet.

ELVIS:
The Philistines may prove a handful.

COLONEL TOM PARKER:
A crock full, son--a crock of cocks! Ha! Ha! The Philistines are *pricks*. When they drop their dicks thou shall prick their pricks. Ha! Ha! Thou wilt become a mighty *Mohel!* (THE COLONEL PULLS OUT ANOTHER CIGAR.) I shall deliver the members to thy hand. You simply stretch the foreskins well past the glans and then...

(The COLONEL clips off the end off the cigar.)

COLONEL TOM PARKER (CONT'D):
Nothing to it, really.

ELVIS:
I'm not sure, Colonel. I don't think I can do this...

COLONEL TOM PARKER:
I've assembled the anxious two-hundred. The hospital staff will assist you in the surgeries. A sharpened sword has been laid upon the altar's stone.

ELVIS:
Can we give them something for the pain?

COLONEL TOM PARKER:
Why of course, E--surgery this slight is *Commedia*. (HE LIGHTS HIS CIGAR) Leave terror to the Turks.

> (ELVIS stands next to a large metal plate on an altar. DOCTOR KOPEL plays the first of the unfortunate Philistines. He walks to the altar stone.)

COLONEL TOM PARKER (CONT'D):
Why it's Lennie! Doctor, I didn't know you were numbered among the elite of Canaan. E, this Philistine is anything but! He's an artist of the first order and entitled to the best care we can offer...

DOCTOR KOPEL:
The medical community is decidedly split...

COLONEL TOM PARKER:
Yes, yes, Doctor "on the medical necessity." Just drop your dong on the gong.

> (DOCTOR KOPEL turns from the audience.)

SOUND CUE: LOUD UNZIPPING SOUND)

> (ELVIS raises his sword high in the air and brings it crashing down upon the Altar plate!)

DOCTOR KOPEL (SCREAMING):
Owwwwwwwwwwwwweeeeeeeeeeeeeeeeeeeeeeeeeeeeeeeeeeeeeeeee!

(KOPEL slowly lurches off stage.)

COLONEL TOM PARKER:
Elvis, that was a touch off the mark--please take a closer aim with the estimable DOCTOR ENGEL. We don't want our offerings to appear mean-spirited.

DOCTOR ENGEL:
Frankly, Stein--the surgery is pointless.

(STEIN turns his back to the audience. Unzipping sound.

COLONEL TOM PARKER:
Try not to cut more than the King can modestly masticate...

(Once again, ELVIS raises the blade...
DOCTOR ENGEL'S member makes a
considerable gong dropping to the sacrificial plate.

ELVIS lowers the sword!)

DOCTOR ENGEL/VERNON (SCREAMING):
Owwwwwwwwwwwwweeeeeeeeeeeeeeeeeeeeeeeeeeeeeeeeeeeeeeeee!

COLONEL TOM PARKER:
Use no yeast. The prepuces must remain unleavened. When baked they have a tendency to rise and this could prove unseemly. Therefore bring the waters of Babylon to a roiling boil.

NURSE MCCARREN:
Doctor Stein, it's the Presley still-born. He's revived!

(NURSE MCCARREN places the baby
JESSE wrapped in swaddling clothes on
the sacrificial plate. ELVIS lets his sword
fall to the floor.

ELVIS/STEIN;
Jesse, he's alive, alive!

COLONEL TOM PARKER:
"sit thyself down and weep, as thou remembers Zion. Happy shall be he that taketh and dasheth thy little ones against the stones."

ELVIS:
Colonel, it's my baby brother...

COLONEL TOM PARKER:
"against the stones", son. Elvis, you can no more share your glory with Jesse than you'll share the bodacious Bathsheba with her husband, Uriah -- ergo, Jesse must die!

ELVIS:
You can't ask that of me!

COLONEL TOM PARKER:
I asked it of Abraham.

ELVIS:
Colonel, Isaac was spared!

COLONEL TOM PARKER:
That was on a Friday, boy--red meat was forbidden me. Your lust is little different than my hunger. Both are voracious and must be sated to be satisfied.

ELVIS:
No, Colonel.

COLONEL TOM PARKER:
You defy me, boy?

ELVIS:
Yes, Colonel.

COLONEL TOM PARKER:
Step aside from that blade! My *appetite enhancer* has just kicked into overdrive...

(The COLONEL retrieves the sword and raises it   aloft)

ELVIS AND PRISCILLA:
Nooooooooooooooooooooooooooooooooooooooooooooooo!

> (ELVIS blocks the ropping blade as NURSE MCCARREN breaks the IV-bottle across the Colonel's head. **(SOUND OF BREAKING GLASS)** The COLONEL drops the sword and collapses into:

QUICK DARKNESS.

SCENE: 3

LIGHTS SLOWLY UP.

PRISCILLA:
Elvis, I had an awful nightmare.

ELVIS:
I know, Cilla. I had it too.

PRISCILLA:
The same dream?

ELVIS:
Yes, Cilla--the same dream. It was the Colonel's nightmare. He's dying, Cilla. He's dying and so are we.

PRISCILLA:
Now *you're* scaring me. Seeing you again, of course, could only be a dream--but I was certain that I was at the other end of it--asleep, somewhere in the Hilton.

ELVIS:

I've been dead for twenty years. But this emptiness is deeper than my own. It's *his*, Cilla and it's becoming hungrier--in the end, it will swallow us all. I don't know where we are--but I'm beginning to think it's not the Hilton.

COLONEL TOM PARKER:

Elvis, might I have a word with you? It's about your pappy. There was some confusion at the altar stone--a mix up between Doctor Engel and Vernon. It seems your daddy came between you and your blade. He's become a trifle unhinged since his hinge fell off the barnyard door--you know the drill: "Eddie Rex has lost his sex so mind your *Pee-Ps and Qs.*"

ELVIS:

Colonel, that was a dream.

COLONEL TOM PARKER:

Well son, a dream is one thing to the dreamer and another to a two-bit piece of peckerwood that's come up a little short in his pocket change. You can take that up with Vernon, but I wouldn't be playing mumbling-peg with your pappy anytime soon.

COLONEL TOM PARKER (CONT'D):

Elvis, Priscilla looks a little *down in the mouth*. Why don't you score her a little Demerol--it will keep her going.

ELVIS:

Demerol? Colonel, the Demerol stopped me cold...

PRISCILLA (SINGSONG, LIKE A CHILD'S RHYME, WHILE SHE HOP-SCOTCHES): The Demmies dulled me down and the dexies pulled me back / You led me to your castle and you tied me to a rack / A pill to make me happy and a pill to make me ball / You never saw the handwriting, scratched upon the wall /

(PRISCILLA regresses to herself as a child.)

PRISCILLA:

Daddy, please come home. I'll be good, I promise. It's Prissy, daddy-- don't let them take me; I'll be good--it's dark, please, don't leave me in the dark...

(PRISCILLA begins to cry she dries her eyes.)

PRISCILLA (SINGS: *DON'T BE CRUEL*):
Baby if I made you mad / with something that I might have said / let's forget about the past 'cause the future looks bright ahead....a few short months...

PROJECT
ELVIS & PRISCILLA, NEWLY WED
APPENDIX 11

PRISCILLA (CONT'D):
Elvis and I adrift--we are shades, lost among the shadows. Pharmaceuticals and fornication——the pills you've gone to fetch were prescribed for a dying old man. Elvis felt it, I feel it, and even Vernon's had a breakdown. The Colonel's scared of the quiet closing in around him and he'll roar like a *she-bear* to keep the emptiness at bay--until in a certainty of silence there's nothing left for him to say.

SCENE 4:

> COLONEL in his wheelchair, bound in his strait-jacket. He begins to wheeze. The wheezing intensifies. It grows louder and louder. The COLONEL gasps to hold on to each breath as if it might be his last. NURSE MCCARREN enters. She frantically looks about for an inhaler.

COLONEL TOM PARKER:
Heehee, heehee, heehee, heehee, heeheeeeeee...

> (She places an inhaler under one nostril than the other. She places a compress on his forehead.

NURSE MCCARREN (OVER THE WHEEZING):
What's been going on in here? Where's Dr. Stein. Something's got you worked up and there's broken glass everywhere! That's better, Colonel--slow and easy, slow and easy.

DARKNESS

(A TITLE CARD IS PROJECTED):

THE BROTHERS KARAMAZOV

NURSE MCCARREN READING (VO):
"And if it is true that children must share responsibility for their fathers' crimes, such a truth is beyond my comprehension. Some jester will say, perhaps, that the child would have grown up and have sinned, but you see he didn't grow up--he was still-born, abandoned, dashed to death upon stones or torn to pieces by... **or torn to pieces by dogs.***"*

(**SOUND CUE:** GROWLING DOG IN DARKNESS

PROJECT
ELVIS & COVER OF THE GRAND INQUIRER
APPENDIX 12

COLONEL TOM PARKER (VO):
Elvis, the insurance providers of the Presley Estate have asked me to make you available for a medical exam--purely routine. Doctor Kopel will conduct his evaluation in the 16th century. Your appointment has been confirmed and conduct to Court of Henry the VIII has been vouchsafed and will be provided. Hall's *Chronicle* is instructive. Please stir clear of the King's mistress, Ann. She's a saucy squeeze but she's the King's squeeze and thou will be served not to want the wanton!

SCENE 5:

MUSIC CUE: Henry VIII's *En Vray Amoure* is played in the darkness.

LIGHT CUE: LIGHTS SLOWLY UP.

VERNON (as King Henry VIII) and PRISCILLA (as Anne Boleyn) who are frozen in mid-dance step. ELVIS, as a court minstrel observes from STAGE LEFT. DOCTOR KOPEL, as CARDINAL THOMAS WOLSEY, observes from STAGE RIGHT. They unfreeze and dance. The *En Vray Amour* concludes and they take their seats.

KING HENRY:
Minstrel--a song!

(ELVIS picks up a lute.
MUSIC CUE: LUTE SOLO)

(He strums a few phrases then grabs PRISCILLA and launches into:

MUSIC CUE: *Bosa Nova Baby*

ELVIS (SINGING & DANCING WITH PRISCILLA):
I said, 'Take it easy, baby
I worked all day and my feet feel just like lead
You got my shirt tails
Flyin' all over the place
And the sweat poppin' out of my head'

She said,
'Hey, Bossa nova, baby
Keep on a workin' child
This ain't no time to quit'
She said, 'Go, Bossa nova, baby
keep on dancin'
I'm about to have myself a fit'
Bossa nova, Bossa nova

ELVIS (SINGING CONT'D)

I said, 'Hey little mama,
Let's sit down
Have a drink and dig the band'
She said, 'Drink, drink, drink
Oh, fiddle-de-dink
I can dance with a drink in my hand'
She said 'Hey Bossa nova, baby
Keep on workin' child
This ain't no time to drink'
She said 'Go, Bossa nova, baby
Keep on dancin'
'Cause I ain't got time to think'

She said, 'Come on, baby
It's hot in here
And it's oh so cool outside
If you lend me a dollar
I can buy some gas
And we can go for a little ride'
She said, 'Hey Bossa nova, baby
Keep on workin' child
I ain't got time for that'
She said, 'Go Bossa nova, baby
Keep on dancin'
Or I'll find myself another cat'

(THE FORMER DOCTOR KOPEL IS
TRANSFORMED INTO CARDINAL
WOLSEY. HE WEARS ROBES AND
HEADGEAR.)

CARDINAL WOLSEY (POINTING):
Guards!

(ELVIS raises his hand to stop the unseen
guards.)

MUSIC CUE: *KYRIE ELESION*

(Choral *KYRIE ELESION* (Part 3 of the KYRIE). WOLSEY/KOPEL approaches the recalcitrant minstrel. ELVIS holds his ground. WOLSEY raises his arm as if to strike him. Something in the singer's demeanor catches the CARDINAL in mid-strike. Thinking better of it the CARDINAL simply bows and gestures ELVIS to the wings.

The DOCTOR begins his exit. He stops. He turns and stares after the now departed ELVIS. He ponders for a beat or two. He turns and exits. DARKNESS. Music continues. LIGHTS SLOWLY UP on the stage. Prison bars are projected on the rear scrim. ELVIS sits at a table. The CARDINAL enters. Music concludes.)

CARDINAL WOLSEY:

We apologize for the accommodations. The guards did not harm you?

ELVIS:

No, Doctor--

CARDINAL WOLSEY:

Cardinal, Mr. Presley. Cardinal Thomas Wolsey. Like the great Abelard before me I took up the Cloth after an accident with a scalpel rendered me especially well-suited to the Priesthood-- once I did things my way--now I do them *Yahweh*. The medical title preceded the Ecclesiastic. I have been blessed to honor God and King in both capacities but my great love is and will continue to be this island's noble horticulture (HE HOLDS UP AN ENGLISH HOTHOUSE CUCUMBER) The Divine Cucumber! It is one sterling reason why we in Britannia assert that God is an Englishman! I grew this in my garden at Hampton Court. Now this odd leaf is tobacco, a Spanish export fresh from the New World. I'm told that the savages smoke the leaf--which is, of course, insufferable. However, when chopped, emulsified and dried

(MORE)

147

CARDINAL WOLSEY (CONT'D):
it makes this delicate, white powder--a miracle elixir that stimulates organs that have long been lost to stimulation.(SNIFF, SNIFF) Would you care for a pinch? As you will. By and large we English remain a civilized lot, thus there is no call for barbarity; this is, after all, a Renaissance. After your internment it was believed you would return to Graceland trailing clouds of Glory--a detail suggestive of another *King,* in another time.

ELVIS:
Doctor, I'm afraid. This place wasn't in the script.

CARDINAL WOLSEY:
That's right, Mr. Presley--the Colonel suggested we take the elevator down a floor or two.

ELVIS:
I don't understand, Doctor.

CARDINAL WOLSEY:
You will, sir--clarity is the reward of patience and its promise. You and I both know that you could easily bring these walls down around our ears, if that were your ...

ELVIS:
Disposition?

CARDINAL WOLSEY:
Precisely...

(The CARDINAL inhales through his right nostril.)

CARDINAL WOLSEY (CONT'D):
Your arrival at the King's Carnival on the first day of Jubilee is certainly extraordinary, albeit...

ELVIS:
Inconvenient?

CARDINAL WOLSEY:

Just so... when the word *is* flesh the spirit weakens.

PROJECT
CHURCH RELICS & FOLDED HANDS
APPENDIX 13

CARDINAL WOLSEY (CONT'D)

At present, here and on the continent, there are 24 hands from the mummified remains of the blessed St. Peter, as to his feet I gave up the count when they exceeded those of a blistered battalion. On any given Sabbath you can light a candle before the head of John the Baptist, two of whose skulls even here, in our...

PROJECT
CATACOMBS & SKULLS
APPENDIX 14

CARDINAL WOLSEY (CONT'D):

Abbey, are prominently on display. You begin, no doubt, to receive my meaning. The mathematics is flagrantly askew! I have, on occasion; purchased fresh milk procured from the Virgin Mary and made celestial omelets from eggs laid by the Holy Ghost when descended as a dove. It was further asserted that the feathers in my plume were plucked from its downy behind upon its return into the heavens. Here you see its lovely feathers are a field...

PROJECT
DOVE ASCENDING
APPENDIX 15

CARDINAL WOLSEY (CONT'D):

and aflutter. To what end, you might ask, are these frauds allowed their petty commerce? And I answer:

COLONEL TOM PARKER (FROM WHEELCHAIR):

Power and Commodity!

CARDINAL WOLSEY:
The church takes 50%. That's right, Mr. Presley, the Colonel was peculiarly adamantine on this very point...

COLONEL TOM PARKER (FROM WHEELCHAIR):
50% from *every* egg laid and *every* ounce milked--Virgin's tit or no.

CARDINAL WOLSEY:
You, however, are a redundancy that will not be permitted!

ELVIS:
I'm tired, Doctor--I just *wanna* go home.

CARDINAL WOLSEY:
Mr. Presley, the stone you rolled away came to rest upon the toe of our Lord and Sovereign, Henry. The times are not propitious to pique a King. Look around. We are at war with the Emperor; and the King's *Neo-cons* wreck havoc from Baghdad to Damascus. The Holy See is sold at auction among the bickering nobility of Rome. The fruit of that remarkable infamy has been prostitution, drunkenness and murder in the Lateran Palace! *This*

> **(The Cardinal slams his fist on the table. The white powder fills the air.)**

CARDINAL WOLSEY (CONT'D):
is your Church! What has been built upon a rock might be better suited slithering back under one.

ELVIS:
My momma always said that the Church was built by hands but the *Word* was whispered only to the heart.

CARDINAL WOLSEY:
The heart is a luxury that we can ill afford. The *Prince* of Machiavelli is not the Prince of Peace--but of Power. Power is not a consequence of prayer but rather deceit, strategy and the sword! Into this cauldron you have chosen to Gavotte and all that

COLONEL TOM PARKER (CONT'D):
you offer is a tender lyric of the heart. It is a lyric not found in my heart, the Colonel's heart or in the heart of any Prince of church or state who desires to remain one! Parker has secured for you employment.   On Good Friday, next -- the Cathedral of the martyred Becket will hold a community barbecue and *Passion*. You will play the *Lamb*...

> (The CARDINAL inhales the long white
> line he's been working on.)

CARDINAL WOLSEY (CONT'D):
SNIFFFFFFFFFFFF--

COLONEL TOM PARKER (RISING):
... the goddamn leg of lamb!

> ELVIS confronts the CARDINAL and the
> COLONEL:

MUSIC CUE: *TROUBLE:*

> (ELVIS and the CARDINAL alternate verses as
> listed below. ELVIS sings the first line; the
> CARDINAL, the second; and the COLONEL,
> the third. The trio forms a chorus line for the
> chorus.)

ELVIS & CARDINAL (SINGING):
ELVIS: *If you're looking for trouble, you've come to the right place* / CARDINAL: *If you're looking for trouble, just get right in my face* / ELVIS: *I was born standing up and talking back* / CARDINAL: *My daddy was a green-eyed mountain jack!* / COLONEL: *So I'M evil, my middle name is misery* / *Yes I'm evil, so don't you mess around with me* /

ELVIS & CARDINAL (CONT SINGING):
ELVIS: *I've never looked for trouble, but I never ran* / CARDINAL: *I don't take no orders from no kind of man* / ELVIS: *I'm only made out of flesh, blood and bone* / COLONEL: *But if you're gonna start a rumble don't you try it on your own.*

CARDINAL (SINGING IN UNISON):
Because I'M evil, my middle name is misery / Well I'm evil, so don't you mess around with me... /

(The COLONEL returns to his
wheelchair.)

CARDINAL WOLSEY:
From lamb to cur, soon all of Canterbury will hear you whimper--
You ain't nothing but a... (PAUSE) you ain't nothing.

ELVIS:
The Colonel promised to help me--to help me find my mother.

CARDINAL WOLSEY:
It is under the Colonel's auspices that you have been condemned. He has washed his hands of you. It matters not whether you're a musical monster cobbled together from the fetid tissue of the Colonel's dementia or if you are in fact, Doctor Terrance Stein, the wayward Oxford wunderkind! I shall take no small pleasure in directing you the dagger's edge. The elevation to the North will be your Golgotha. Sufficient wine will be provided. (A FINAL SNIFF ON THE INHALER) Pray it prove more an anesthetic than was offered to me.

> **DARKNESS**
> SOUND: CHORAL BACH'S CRUCIFIXUS AND
> SOUND: HAMMER BLOWS.
>
> **MUSIC CUE**: Mass in B Minor.
> Choir continues in darkness.

**PROJECT
GRUENWALD'S MOURNERS AT CROSS
APPENDIX 16**

(Lights slowly up. ELVIS IS ON CROSS in background. NURSE MCCARREN and DOCTOR ENGEL attend the diminishing COLONEL.)

NURSE MCCARREN:
... 210/170--Doctor, 250 and its still rising!

DOCTOR ENGEL:
Methyldolpa, now! Stein, page Doctor Kopel!

NURSE MCCARREN:
Doctor, I can't find a vein!

(DARKNESS - EXIT NURSE AND DOCTOR
LIGHTS SLOWLY UP ON THE CRUCIFIED
ROCK STAR)

SCENE 6:

COLONEL TOM PARKER:
Elvis...

ELVIS (REVIVING):
Yesssssssssss?

COLONEL TOM PARKER:
Son, it's the Colonel.

ELVIS:
Colooooonel--I've made a mess... a mess of things--tell Priscilla I love her--forgive her your 50%, she knows nnnnnot what she does.

COLONEL TOM PARKER:
Her ignorance will not save either of you. She is as unfaithful as you and, like your pappy, a thief to boot. Had I my druthers she'd be nailed to a cross beam on your left and he'd be dangling on your right!

(The COLONEL begins wrapping a rubber tube around his arm. He is trying to tease a vein into view.)

COLONEL TOM PARKER:
You think that's unduly harsh of me and perhaps, crucifying the dead is a gesture fraught with futility. But there are precedents and son, this is *the* Passion that redeems your world.

(The COLONEL taps at a vein in his forearm.)

COLONEL TOM PARKER (CONT'D):
This? This ain't *Jack*!... This is the passion that redeems mine. Wait a second, there she be, come on little fellah, I won't hurt you (HE SHOOTS UP) ahhhhhhhhhhhhhh--a heart medication--ain't that a kick in the balls! --me with a heart problem! (BREATHING DEEPLY) Yes that's better,(PAUSE) much   better. Always remember, E, "you don't have to be nice to folks on the way up unless you plan on meeting them on the way down" and I'm not going down!

ELVIS:
Nails--nailed my hannns.

COLONEL TOM PARKER:
Skeweers? That, of course, is essential to the book, my cook book*!*

ELVIS:
I'm scared, Colonel. Can you hhhhhelp... me...

COLONEL TOM PARKER:
Sorry, son--that was the last of my stash.

ELVIS:
Colonel, the cra, cra, crosss? Whhhhhhhhhhy?

COLONEL TOM PARKER:
The Cross is the lynch pin of creation. It is punishment both at its nadir and apogee. Put simply, the cross is a chrysalis--you and Jesse are the butterflies pinioned at its center. Yes, I'm afraid the *Evils* in the anagram of Elvis are as necessary as the Jesus in the benefaction of Jesse--a cemetery of symmetry, a universe of death over which, you, my pet, will shortly soon preside. No mere mortal can restrain the voice of a whirlwind and the voice of *the Whirlwind* is mine! You say that I held you back. You say that I took more than 50% of what you earned. You took 50% of what *I* mother-fucking earned! The documents you and your family signed have returned the controlling interest in Presley Enterprises to its proper executor. Damn you... Goddamn you all for attempting to *Hoodwink* Colonel Thomas Parker. (BREATHING HEAVILY--PAUSE) You squandered a talent rarely bequeathed. In the end you betrayed only yourself. In searching for the face of Jesus, you've discovered the face of Judas, to be your own.

EPILOGUE:

NURSE MCCARREN"
And what of the face of Andreas? You've spent a lifetime playing God, now Colonel, you must think back to when you were merely a man——Andreas Cornelis van Kuikj. Thou canst not pour new wine into old bottles. This is the first lesson of *two* that I will grant you this day. Yes Colonel, what of Andreas and more tellingly, what of Anna?

COLONEL (NOW THROUGH CONCLUSION WITH DUTCH ACCENT):
Loanne?

NURSE MCCARREN:
Long before Loanne, there was your first Anna--Anna van den Enden, wife of Jan van den Enden. You were dismissed from the army in 1932 after treatment for mental aberration. Do you remember the diagnosis?

COLONEL TOM PARKER(CONJURING MEMORY):
That was a long time ago...

NURSE MCCARREN:
"Clinical Psychopathology--delusions of grandeur in extremis."
Death is stalking you, Colonel--death for death. They said you were
crazy and then they discharged you! Think, Andreas the 17th of
May-1927, the day you abandoned your family and fled your native
Holland.

CARDINAL WOLSEY:
For the crimes of witchcraft, incest and adultery--our Lord and
Liege Henry, 8th King of that name and Supreme Head of the
Church in England, pronounces death upon Anne Boleyn, death
upon Anna van den Enden, death upon Priscila Beaulieau, and yes-
-death upon the father and death upon the son, death to God
almighty and death to everyone!

> HE GENUFLECTS
> ENTER PRISCILLA (as ANNA),
> STAGE RIGHT.

ANNA VAN DEN ENDEN:
Jan, is that you...

COLONEL TOM PARKER:
Anna, it is Dreas.

> (ENTER the COLONEL from STAGE LEFT.)

ANNA VAN DEN ENDEN:
Andreas, you should not be here--Jan will soon return.

COLONEL TOM PARKER:
Tonight, Anna I leave for America. I said I would come for you.
Now, Anna, true to my word--I have come--

ANNA VAN DEN ENDEN:
Listen to me Andreas. I married Jan. He is my husband. I am
making *his* dinner. I love him and only him.

COLONEL TOM PARKER:
Anna please, I have passage for two, *ik ben alleen* "I'm alone..."

ANNA VAN DEN ENDEN(WITH WINE BOTTLE):
I pity you, Dreas--now you must go and I must marinate the lamb...

(The COLONEL touches her shoulder
as reaches around to break her neck.)

ANNA VAN DEN ENDEN:
Dreas...

DARKNESS

ANNA VAN DEN ENDEN (VO, SCREAMING)
Owwwwwwwwwweeeeeeeeeeeeeeeeeee!

SILENCE
LIGHTS UP

(ELVIS on the cross and the COLONEL
are alone at Center Stage and frozen in a
grim tableau. The COLONEL turns to
the unconscious ELVIS, touches his
nailed feet and begins to sing through his
sobs.)

COLONEL TOM PARKER (SINGING):
Hush little baby don't you cry / You know
your daddy's ...

(ELVIS awakens on the cross.)

ELVIS:
Momma--Momma, is that you mah, mah,
ahhhhhhhhhhhhhhhh...

(ELVIS slumps and dies. The COLONEL
removes his hat and falls to his knees, he starts to
slowly wheeze. BACH takes to his podium,

DOCTOR ENGEL holds a CANDLE adjacent to the Kapellmeister. The COLONEL'S wheezing rises to a fever pitch and then quiets & allows him his final words.

COLONELPARKER (WITH A THICK DUTCH BROGUE)
Heeeheehe--Mijn God--I am alone,
Ik ben alleen in the
darkkkkkkkkkkkkkkkkkkkkkkkkkkkkkkkkkkkkkkkkkkkkk...

HE DIES
LIGHT CUE: QUICK DARKNESS-
ONLY THE CANDLE ILLUMINATES

MUSIC CUE: BACH BEGINS
CONDUCTING
THE DONA NOBIS PACEM.

The "interrupted" music of the ***GRATIA AGIMUS TIBI***, from the end of Act I, now repeats and moves to completion: On the rear scrim is projected:

PROJECT
COLONEL TOM PARKER IN HAT AND CIGAR
JUNE 26, 1909 - JANUARY 21, 1997
APPENDIX 17

Actors Kopel, Engle and Stein place lit candles upon an altar beneath the screen. The date fades.

PROJECT
ELVIS ARON PRESLEY
JANUARY 8, 1935 – AUGUST 16,1977
APPENDIX 18

AS THE MUSIC CONTINUES A TITLE CARD IS PROJECTED OF
THE KING'S STATIONS OF THE CROSS:

UNION STATIONS:
Memphis Tenn.

TRAIN TO GRACELAND
PROCESSION - APOTHEOSIS

THREE PANELS
ARE PROJECTED IN TURN:

TO GRACELAND

PROCESSION

APOTHEOSIS

NURSE MCCARREN WALKS TO THE LAST
PHOTO.
SHE HOLDS A CANDLE UP TO EXAMINE THE
BACK OF HER FINGERS.
SHE PUTS THE CANDLE ON THE ALTAR
SHE EXITS.

THE FINAL PANEL ILLUMINATES TO A
BLINDING BRILLIANT WHITE...

The Music Concludes.

Darkness
&
Curtain

END

POSTLUDE:

SOUND CUE # 15:
Presley recording
of
Viva Las Vegas

.

APPENDIX

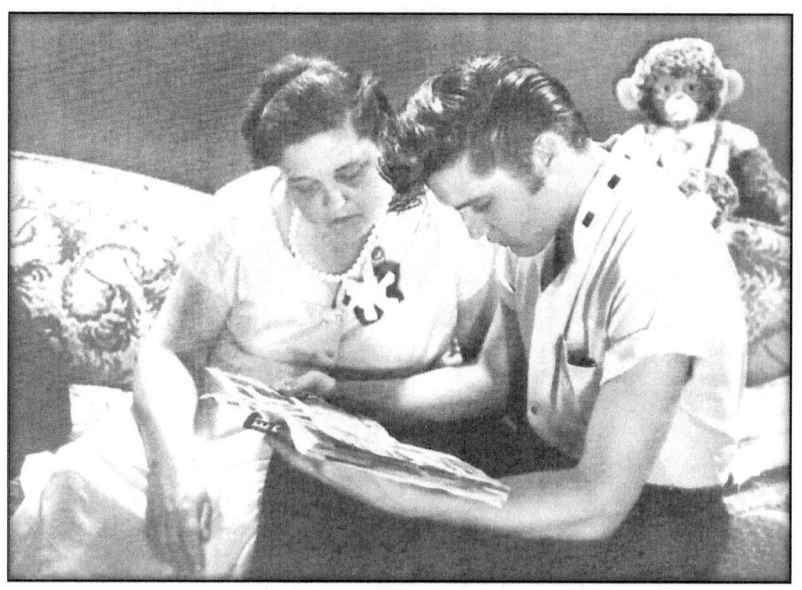

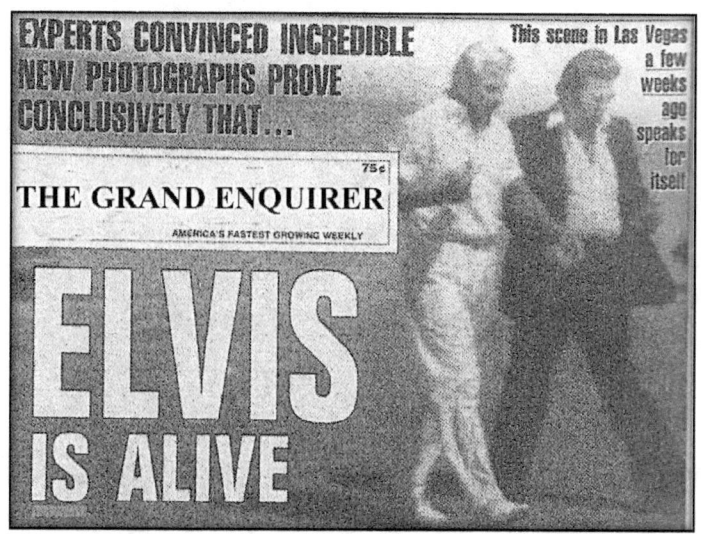

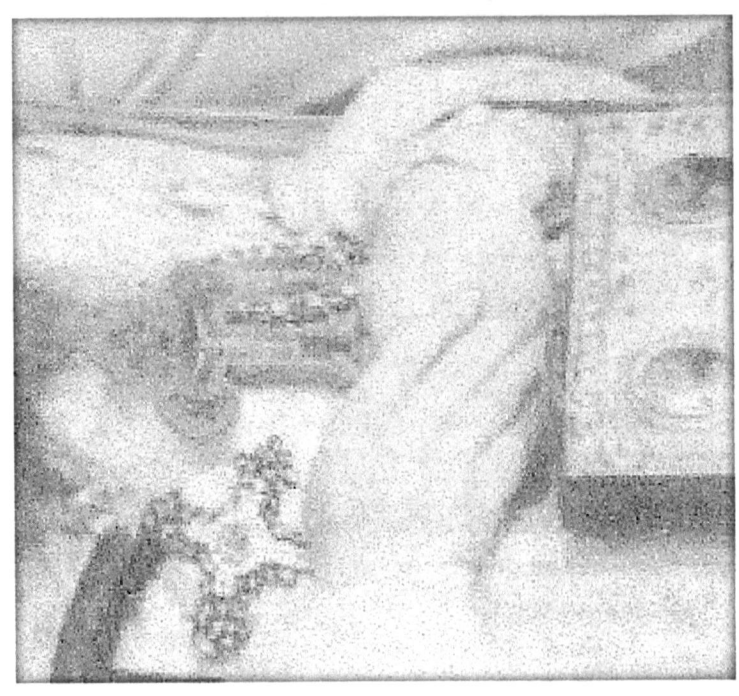

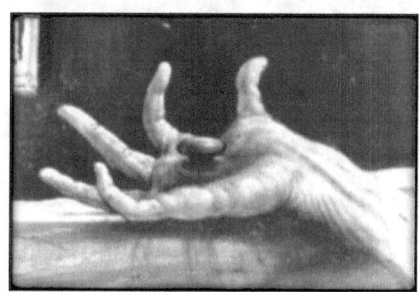

THEOPHANY

PICTURE CREDITS
of
E & E

Photographs for *The Man From Lloyds* appear primarily as a courtesy of Google Images. Jean Jules Verdenal is an enigma and an everyman—his photo was selected from a group of anonymous French soldiers circa Spring of 1915.

Photographs for *A Presley Passion* also appear as a courtesy of Google images. Mention should be made of Appendix photos 8, 10, and Theophany—these three photos were gleaned from the collection of Jim Curtain: *Unseen Elvis, Candids of the King.* Jim must have lifted a family album— you'll find fistfuls of photos not likely viewed elsewhere.

The photography has been assembled as a suggestive point of departure.
Each production is free to find its way.

www.ingramcontent.com/pod-product-compliance
Lightning Source LLC
Chambersburg PA
CBHW050939120626
46552CB00001B/284